AIR
WHISPERERS
OF
NKANDLA

ISBN Soft Cover, 978-0-473-41313-2
ISBN Kindle, 978-0-473-41314-9

AIR

WHISPERERS

OF

NKANDLA
PATRICIA PIKE

eshwity

Publishers

www.reshwit

y.wixsite.com/patriciapike

GLOSSARY

Kraal: Group of huts where a family unit lives often surrounding a secure place for the family cattle to be gathered.

Sanibona: Greeting to a group of people in Zulu.

Tshwala beer: Homemade beer.

U'Bantu: People of Africa.

Assegai: Short stabbing spear.

Suthu: People of Lesotho, a mountain kingdom near Zululand.

Kalisnikov rifle: Assault rifle.

Sangoma: Zulu witchdoctor.

Bulala: Command to kill or murder.

Lammergeyer: Large eagle capable of capturing a small animal.

Sonne g'Nyoga: Zulu curse meaning 'Son of a snake.'

Boma: Usually made from thorn tree branches overlaid to form an impenetrable containment for animals or people.

Rusk: Hard bread used for trail food and baby's teething.

Calabash: Water casket made from dried squash.

Putu: Maize based staple food cooked and eaten with variety of sauces.

Swazi karosse: Woollen or animal hide blanket with a distinctive design peculiar to the Swazi people incorporating different animal skins sewn together.

Madumbes: (Colocasi esculenta) Zulu potato similar to the Taro plant of Polynesia.

Beshu: Animal skin loin covering worn by men and boys.

Gogo: Old, honoured person.

Kloof: Steep sided ravine or valley.

Tagahti: Curse placed on an activity or person.

Hambane Gahle: Farewell greeting meaning go well.

Guibourtia Tessmannii Bubinga tree: Extremely expensive and rare Central African wood.

CAST OF CHARACTERS

Atalia: (means 'God is Great' in Hebrew) Mother of the young king Eric. Wife to previous Zulu king.

Thandi: (tan di) (means 'loving one' in Zulu) Air Whisperer and wife to Alpheus able to transform into petals and smaller particles lifted and transported by air.

Alpheus: (meaning 'learned chief') Male head of the family.

Ragnar: (meaning 'strong counselor' in Norse) Orphan taken in by Zulu king.

Nyoni: (in yo nee) (meaning 'bird' in Zulu) Senior wife of Alpheus and able to transform into birds.

Sandra: Youngest wife of Alpheus and has various skills of air walking.

Raz: Captain in the Zulu king's guard.

Phoebe: Eldest daughter of Alpheus and Nyoni.

Eric: King of the Zulus.

Ndlovu: (in doh lo vu) (means 'elephant' in Zulu) Chief of the elephant people.

Izzie: Matriarch of the elephant people.

Tembe: Eldest daughter of Ndlovu and Izzie.

Sipho: (means 'gift' in Zulu) Eldest son of Alpheus and Thandi.

Rachel: Younger daughter of Alpheus and Thandi.

E'showe: (ee sho wee) (sound of wind through the trees) Aged chieftain of the forest people.

Namaqua: (nam ak wa) (meaning 'long tailed dove' in the Nama language) School friend of Eric and daughter of Nkomo and Nyama.

Nkomo: (in corm oh) (means 'cow' in Zulu) Beef baron and friend of Atalia.

Nyama: (in yam a) (means 'meat' in Zulu) Wife of Nkomo and mother of Namaqua.

Perseus: School friend of Eric and nemesis of Ragnar, often called Per by his friends.

Xele: (teh lee) (means 'widening' in Zulu, probable a nickname because he is tall and thin, so he was named for the polar opposite of his looks) Elephant soldier, trainer, grey eyed.

Isifunda: (is i foon dah) (means 'I have learnt' in Zulu) Elephant soldier, master of stealth. Spectacles and muscled.

Bala: (baa laa) (means to 'calculate' in Zulu) Elephant soldier with scarred face.

Maria: Young daughter of Alpheus and Thandi

Cedric: Older brother to King Eric, who lives in Paris with his partner

Francis: Partner to Prince Cedric

Claude: Older brother to King Eric, who lives in Switzerland.

Place Names

Zululand: Ancient kingdom in southern Africa.

Nkandla: (in carn dla) Small village amongst a spiritual forest revered by the Zulu people.

Mtunzini: (im toon zee nee) Village overlooking a lagoon filled with crocodiles and abundant wildlife.

Lesotho: (Leh sue too) Mountain kingdom on the southern edge of Zululand.

Melmoth: Farming village at the top of a mountain pass.

Swaziland: Mountain kingdom to the north of Zululand.

Mozambique: (Mo zam beak) Large country to the north.

Kwa Dlangezwa: (kwah da lang gehs wa) University town.

Ubombo: (you bomb oh) sacred mountain where great chieftains are buried, south of Swaziland.

FOREWORD

In Africa polygamy is a common practise and has been part of the culture for thousands of years. When practised correctly it can be a very mutually beneficial relationship for all involved. Unfortunately, this is not always the case. If you are involved or know someone involved in a romantic relationship where anyone is abused then help should be sort after. The relationships depicted in this story are fictional but is meant to represent the cultural norms of Africa where polygamy is still practised.

PART ONE:
EXODUS OF NKANDLA

PROLOGUE

Atalia held the syringe in her hand and watched as the poison she had injected into the IV, dripped slowly into the vein of the king. She put a cool hand on his fevered brow and hummed softly. "Sleep my king, sleep the sleep of eternity."

No guilt and no pity for the man who now lay writhing on the bed. His eyes opened and he lifted a hand towards his wife.

"Help me, Atalia, the room is getting dark and the pain is awful, too awful to stand."

She leaned down and kissed him gently on the cheek. "It's time for our son to take the reins of leadership, my liege. You're getting old and foolish. I know you've always been weak. This was inevitable. I'm a conduit to help you on this last journey."

Atalia gazed out the window at the moon in the night sky and smiled as she shook his hand off her arm. She heard his agonized gasps, now well past the effort of speech. A sound like the whimpering of a dog in pain had Atalia whipping around in alarm. Narrowing her eyes, she peered into each nook and cranny, but she could see not anything unusual and shrugged it off. "Perhaps it's a dog crying somewhere." She turned back to view the moon high above.

It had taken years to get the result she wanted. The slow undermining of her stepson's rights to the crown and tutoring her son so he would be the popular choice to inherit the titles and power.

The oldest son had been no problem. His love of fast cars and loose women had given her the incentive to hire a mechanic to tinker with his Mercedes sports car's brakes.

The funeral had taken a whole week and the king had cried on her shoulder for many nights.

The second son was even easier. Firmly ensconced in the city with his male lover. A few photos of the two of them together had convinced her husband this son would not be able to supply the future generations of royal blood.

The second son was given a large settlement in exchange for a signature on the bottom of a binding agreement to never challenge any future kings.

The third son suffered with asthma and allergies. Ground peanuts added a little at a time to his meals meant he was sent away to Switzerland to a special clinic. Where he made a miraculous recovery from all his symptoms.

None of the daughters of the king were any threat to Atalia as she made sure they were married off to princes of other royal houses in Africa. Often their mothers would accompany them to their new homes and this suited Atalia's purposes.

Her son became the focus of the king's affection and the two were often in each other's company as the king oversaw the decisions of his realm. Atalia thought of her son, the future king of Zululand, and how great she could become with him under her control. Rubbing her arms in glee she grinned as her imagination created a life of power and riches beyond measure.

The king lay still on his death bed and Atalia took the time to replace the bag of liquid connected to his drip with an untainted bag. She smoothed the sheets where the king had writhed and twisted them in his death throes. Finally, she eased his eyes closed and composed his body into a semblance of restful sleep.

Checking her lipstick in the mirror she fluffed up her hair before turning to check the room for any evidence of the murder she had committed.

She patted her pocket where the vial of poison lay, the bag of saline solution fitted into the other pocket. Pleased to note it was almost undetectable to anyone who might see her. If she was ever questioned she could always say she was a concerned wife checking on her sick husband. Perfectly normal in the situation.

Taking the incriminating evidence of her perfidy, she slipped past the sleeping guard and back into her own room. The sky showed signs of dawn and Atalia lay down on her own bed, closed her eyes and soon slept the sleep of the justified.

CHAPTER ONE

Thandi stood on the canopy of the giant trees and surveyed all the majesty before her. Tambooti trees swayed in the gentle breeze. She saw her husband, Alpheus, leaning against the fence surveying his cows.

Ten bulls and three cows made no sense to Thandi, but Alpheus thought he was the richest man in Nkandla. If there was a family celebration it would not be a bull slaughtered, but rather one of the fertile cows and Thandi shook her head at the stupidity of it all.

Stepping lightly from one tree top to another, she used them as a means to get lower to the ground like an oversized step ladder. The final step took her down to the gate of the kraal.

Nyoni and Sarah were creating grass baskets wound around in ropes or bands of wrapped grass. Some were dyed and woven into intricate patterns.

Thandi took her place next to the two women. Running her hands over her generous hips. She smoothed a stray string of beads off her brow. As the lightest skinned of the three wives she was often called the white Zulu by her detractors. She didn't care about the teasing, she could give as good as she got.

Some long-forgotten ancestor had strayed to the white side of town for their sexual pleasure and in her, the genes had manifested as pale skin and silky long hair.

Nyoni, Alpheus' other wife, had a helmet of terracotta clay smeared into her hair and this gave Thandi a little thrill of pleasure and pride at her own long locks. Sandra had her hair braided with multi coloured beads creating a tinkle of sound as she walked. Not ideal for stalking people or animals but certainly very pretty. Thandi loved her fellow wives but she sometimes had to stop herself from feeling superior. If her grandmother knew, she would surely have beaten it out of her many years ago.

Thandi sat down next to the other wives and never showed by the least little smirk she had been sky hopping instead of working. Picking up the basket she had been working on she let her mind drift into pleasant spheres of thought as her fingers wove the intricate patterns. The baskets rose out of the earth into marvellous items of symmetric beauty.

Thandi dreamily peered into the sky and noticed an odd shape drifting over the valley. There were quite a few of them advancing with great plumes of noxious fumes trailing behind them. Their ability to fly above the trees made their passage easy as the forest in Nkandla was dense in some areas.

Thandi clicked her tongue to announce to the other women they had company. Nyoni stood slowly and backed herself into the shadows of the hut behind her. In the twinkling of an eye she metamorphosed into a little sparrow, her helmet of red clay transformed into a few russet coloured feathers dipped and swayed in the breeze. She hopped onto the thatch and flew toward the cattle kraal, alighting on Alpheus' shoulder.

This was Nyoni's right as wife number one, to greet the visitors alongside her husband. Alpheus was a tall, thin man with a sprinkling of grey through tightly curled hair. Hidden under his brightly coloured shirt were a set of impressive muscles honed by hours spent with fighting sticks and imaginary foes. He might be a middle-aged man, but many a young buck had learned to respect him as he firmly put them in their place when they challenged his seniority.

Alpheus squinted his eyes into the glare of the bright summer sky as he focused on the craft.

"Nyoni, take the children into the forest. Now. Don't let the sky soldiers see you." He whispered to the sparrow.

Thandi herded the youngsters into a small group next to the hut, furthest from Alpheus' position. The children ranged from age seventeen to, the latest addition, of a few months old. Thandi strapped the baby to her back and took two little ones by the hand. She nimbly transported them into the tree tops. Nyoni, the senior wife; and Sarah, the youngest, each took a child by the hand and ushered them into the protection of the forest giants.

The airships hovered over their home. Choking them with smoke from the steam-powered ships. Rope ladders were thrown over the edge and men nimbly climbed down.

Alpheus strode towards the place where ten, leather bound, gun toting visitors alighted from their air bikes. They were also steam-powered but had the body of a motorbike on steroids. Alpheus felt the comforting bump of his fighting stick against his hip and smiled quietly to himself.

"Sanibona. How are you today, travellers? Welcome to my home and how can I be of service?"

For all Alpheus' smile and jovial manner, his hand was never far from the carved stick at his side.

The closest soldier spat on the ground before he spoke. "We've heard your family can walk the skies without needing contraptions." He motioned with his head to indicate their own vehicles. "They can reach places in silence many of us would like to visit. Fetch the ladies, now, so we can talk." The punk grinned exposing his sharpened teeth and diamond encrusted incisors. His clothing covered in vicious looking steel barbs.

Alpheus studied the man closely and thought he was a man with no manners or finesse at all. Surely the visitors should have shown common courtesy and at least enquired as to the health of Alpheus and his family before demanding their attendance.

"Wouldn't you like some tshwala beer, my visitors? Surely you're thirsty. If we could sit like cultured men and have a discussion I'm sure we could come to some agreement."

Alpheus was desperate to distract the men from the family who needed time to escape this potentially violent meeting. Out the corner of his eye Alpheus saw the little sparrow return. A quick glance at the tree tops showed him Thandi settling down with a crossbow in her hands. She focused on the leader using her eagle eye as well as the sighting mechanism on her weapon.

It was only his youngest wife, Sarah, who had not returned and Alpheus hoped she had left to protect the little ones.

The leader growled. "My name is Raz and I'm a captain in the king's army. No, we don't require refreshment and your time is short, for at this very moment I've men searching the forest to find your family. If they're not brought to me I'll start to burn down your huts." He gestured with his rifle.

Raz looked at one of his men and gave him a silent command. The man strode to the cattle kraal and with a flick of his wrist cut the throat of the largest bull. Alpheus forced himself not to react as his prized possession bled out in front of him. The other cattle complained and shuffled against the far barrier of their enclosure.

"A taste of what will happen if you don't comply." Raz sat down on the dusty ground and laid his Kalashnikov rifle across his knees.

Nyoni flew into the tree canopy to discuss their situation with her fellow wife.

Her voice a hushed whisper so they would not be over heard by the searching soldiers. "Thandi what's the best thing to do? I know these men have no qualms in doing as they threatened, but I don't want to cause more injury to our children." They all looked pained at the idea of their children coming to any harm.

"Do you think we should attack? Or surrender?" Neither one was a good option. If they attacked they would be placing themselves against the Zulu king and his soldiers. If they surrendered they would be forced to work as slaves for the Zulu king.

"Personally, I prefer the first option as these thugs will never leave without causing trouble. They look like they enjoy hurting people." Nyoni said the last with her teeth gritted, ready for a fight.

Thandi weighed up the options and decided she would be the one to give herself for a sacrifice to protect the family. The Zulu warriors only needed one Air Whisperer.

"The family need you to lead them, Nyoni and I trust you to look after my children if I'm injured. Plus, I think I've a few tricks up my sleeve to distract Raz the rat." She laughed quietly. "Can you do some damage to the soldiers while I play the vixen? Maybe we should get Phoebe to join you? She's more than capable of helping you out."

Whistling quietly, they called Phoebe from the forest floor and filled her in on their plan. Her eyes shone and a wicked grin changed her face from angel to devil in a second. As the oldest daughter she had come into her Air Whispering powers and capable of protecting herself.

Nyoni returned to her human form and took her place behind the crossbow. Thandi materialised from the darkness of the hut closest to her husband and the visitors.

"Husband, do you require me to entertain the visitors?" Thandi asked politely.

Alpheus scowled. His wives often did things strange to him. Raz was surprised at the sudden appearance of this tall Zulu woman who showed no sign of concern. He motioned for Thandi to entertain him. Thandi hopped over the heads of the men and danced along the fence line of the cattle enclosure.

She skipped and twirled and tumbled through the air, landing lightly on the back of the bull's horns as it lay twitching on the ground. Touching it gently on its head calmed it down as the death throes finally subsided.

One of the men clapped his hands in delight until Raz glared at him and he hung his head at the implied rebuke from his leader.

"Woman, stop this silliness and come here so we can talk about what needs to be done." Raz glowered at Thandi, but she smiled sweetly and hopped off the horns of the bull and landed lightly in front of the thug.

"Anything to please you, great soldier of the king," she whispered seductively, "What's your pleasure?"

"It's not my pleasure, but what you can do for our great ruler. Chief of all uBantu, defender of the weak, hero of the battle of Mtunzini, killer of the giant lion and gracious to all his enemies."

Thandi smiled to herself, thinking it was not how she viewed their illustrious king. King of the large ego, killer of dreams. As to the hero of any battle? The only battle he had ever been part of was when he viewed the dead from the back of a bullet proof vehicle surrounded by hordes of thugs like the ones now gracing their humble home.

Thandi though said without an ounce of sarcasm. "My Lord, you're worthy of so much respect for reminding me of whom I serve. Tell me, what I need to do?"

Raz nodded to one of his henchmen and a folding table was brought forward. A large map was laid out and both

Alpheus and Thandi peered at it. Villages and kraals were coloured with different symbols. Their kraal was marked with a blue spiral. Other kraals were marked with similar symbols, but many of them had black crosses through them.

Only three blue spiral kraals were still active and Alpheus made note of them for future reference. Maybe they could join together with them for safety?

The king's great kraal was marked with brown diamonds on the large map and there were other symbols scattered around the land but neither Alpheus, nor Thandi, knew what they signified.

Alpheus was a great strategist but often relied on his wives to transport him where he wanted to be. He couldn't do this in this situation and looked around at his wife to see if he could read her mind and see what the women had planned. He sighed as he wondered what it would be like to swoop through the air like an eagle or float on a breeze like a feather.

Their abilities to use the air was something gifted to the women only, Alpheus was the father of the next generation of Air Whisperers. But this did not mean Alpheus was not an important part of their lives and it was him who felt the weight of responsibility to keep them all safe.

None of the women were sure what their particular ability would be until they reached the age of womanhood. Some could change into birds, others could influence the weather and the skies, while others had multiple talents.

Each woman would start with at least one gift and then work to harness the powers around them. Nyoni could not only change into various birds, but could control the wind and weather in small areas. Thandi could walk on air as well as change into microscopic particles travelling on the air without being noticed. Sarah so far had only been able to air walk, but she already showed signs of being a great talent in the Air Whisperers' world as she had learned how to speak to birds and started shifting items with her mind.

Busy jabbing his finger onto the map Raz smirked. "The Lesotho kingdom needs to be brought into line with the Zulus. We've tried various times to infiltrate the mountains and to attack and subdue the nation, but the Lesotho were obstinate and noncompliant with the very reasonable request to join with the Zulu king and become his armies. Bayete, our king and queen are great."

Thandi had to stop herself from rolling her eyes at this stupidity, in case Raz or one of his men noticed her disrespect for their esteemed leader.

Alpheus shook his head. "I don't know what you want us to do. None of my women can transport a whole army to the top of a mountain. It'd be too much for even them." Thandi did not contradict her husband although sure between the three women the task could be managed.

Raz straightened and glared at Thandi and Alpheus before he declared. "Yes, but they can create clouds to hide our approach as well as blowing our airships up from the valleys and over the mountain ramparts. Our airships can carry a hundred soldiers each and we have ten airships at our disposal. One thousand trained troops will certainly do the trick." Pleased with himself and his succinct explanation of the strategy, he only revealed his inexperience.

Taking out a clear plastic cover Raz laid it over the map. With a few coloured pens from one of his men, he proceeded to lay out the battle plans. "These kraals will have to be decimated or destroyed. We'll then collect up the cattle and with a few trained cow herders usher them down the mountainsides. Don't worry we'll have them protected by armed soldiers. The final push would be to the Lesotho royal household where the young princesses will be taken as brides for soldiers who have proven themselves brave and loyal."

Raz had a glazed look in his eyes as he contemplated these rewards. His enthusiasm distracted him for a moment from his audience and Alpheus was able to signal Thandi that she should leave. Shaking her head imperceptibly she smiled sweetly at her husband and his frown.

She was waiting for the signal from Nyoni in the treetops to indicate the children were safe.

"My dear, Captain Raz, this plan is certainly impressive, but why do you need us? Surely you've Air Whisperers who are already employed by our illustrious king?" Alpheus asked innocently, knowing full well the other Air Whisperers were slowly dying under the harsh conditions at the palace.

The female Air Whisperers had refused to take husbands and so no new children were born to replace them. Rumours had been blown on the winds over the past few years of terrible atrocities visited upon these beautiful women if they refused to obey the king. They had been raped repeatedly by soldiers on the king's orders.

If the women found themselves pregnant they chose to commit suicide. They would twist ropes around their necks so they would fall to their deaths using the air giving them life, so their children would not be used for nefarious means.

All the women at Alpheus's kraal cried cascades of tears as news of these things reached them. Phoebe, the eldest daughter, had been kept close to home in case she too was kidnapped.

"Why don't the women fly away from the abuse? Why do they stay?" Sarah had sobbed when she had heard the rumours. They all heard about the brothers of these women being held as slaves in the palace dungeons to ensure they complied with the orders. This was why Alpheus decided to stay in the forests of Nkandla in the hope they would be forgotten or overlooked. He knew now this was a pipe dream quickly turning into a nightmare.

Thandi on the other hand tried to find a way to save her husband. Every scenario had a flaw. She had accepted all their material goods would be forfeit to the might of the thugs, but they all needed Alpheus. He hunted for their food, he loved them and cared for them all when they were ill. He was essential to the happiness of the family. Other people might think men were superfluous to the women of the Air Whisperers' tribes, but they were wrong.

Thandi slipped her hand into her husband's and twined her fingers through his. Rubbing her thumb across his fingertips gently, to tell him how much she would miss him if he were not there. He squeezed her hand in acknowledgement.

A shift in the air heralded the arrival of Nyoni, appearing behind one of the soldiers guarding the flying contraptions. With a quick stab, she placed the assegai under his ribs and into his heart, she then transported the body and hung it from a tree. A gruesome mockery of the shrike's habit of storing its food on the thorns of trees. She did this twice more without being noticed by anyone except Thandi and Alpheus.

Seven to three was more manageable, but it didn't account for the troops searching the forests. The soldiers, closer and were within the sight line of Raz and so Thandi leaned forward brushing her breasts against his arm as if by accident. Alpheus rolled his eyes. Aware his wife was merely distracting the man but unsure what her plans were to be.

Raz looked down the front of Thandi's top as she simpered next to him.

"What big muscles you men have." She whispered as she touched his biceps. "Can you tell me more about the attack

of the great Zulu against the weak Suthu, my dear General?"
Exaggerating his rank in flattery.

"What do you want to know? You'll come with us and
control the weather for a day, two at the most, while we
accomplish our goals. Simple things even women can do."

Thandi saw in her peripheral vision Phoebe joining the
fray. Two more men died, without uttering a sound, to be
whisked off to oblivion. Five down. Five to go.

Alpheus saw the men being dealt with behind Raz but he
didn't let it show on his face. When he deemed the odds
were in their favour he hefted his fighting stick between his
hands and with a quick wink to his wife, he twirled around
and brought it crashing down on Raz's body.

He missed the vulnerable head by a hair's breadth and
caught Raz in a blow across the shoulders. With a crack
broke bone and dislocated the shoulder.

Raz roared in anger and pain as he twisted around,
slashing with his good arm. He held a short stabbing spear
in his hand and as he turned he managed to slice Alpheus'
arm to the bone.

Thandi had a soldier by the hair and flew higher as he
screamed in terror. She let him go and he plummeted to the
earth where his screams were cut off. Nyoni had a soldier
dangling from her hands as she flung him high in the air.
She created a wind storm around the remaining two soldiers
leaving them grabbing for a stable hand hold or risk being
blown away.

The three women worked in harmony to blow the
soldiers across the valley and into an area of swamp housing
a monstrous crocodile fond of human flesh. If the soldiers
managed to get out of there alive they would find their
flying machines broken in pieces and face a long walk home.
As Nyoni directed the wind to rip the sails of the airships

and bikes. They teetered on their sides before crashing into the ground.

Raz moaned in agony and scrambled for his Kalashnikov rifle. With a flick of a finger Thandi had it skittering across the ground out of his reach.

Nyoni had a handful of spider webs she quickly packed into Alpheus' wound. She touched Alpheus on the forehead and with a sigh he collapsed into a deep painless sleep. This skill the women took for granted and used all the time to ease the pain of man and beast.

The three women walked towards Raz and stood over him with hands on their hips.

"Should we kill him? Or should we allow him to return to the palace and tell the despot king we're not interested in his schemes?" Nyoni asked in her singsong voice.

"Yes, perhaps we should, but then it means we'll be fugitives in our own land and hiding from our own people forever. We're damned if we let him live and we're damned if we dispose of him." Thandi countered.

"Don't worry, my sister. I have a plan. And it's better to be a fugitive from people like this than to side with them."

Nyoni touched Raz on the head and he too descended into sleep. Nyoni and Thandi each took an arm, not caring it would cause him further agony when he woke up. They created a small whirlwind and they flew into the sky across the land until they could see the village of Melmoth.

Waiting until there were no people in sight, they set down and left him lying on the side of the highway. Their final parting gift was to wake him.

CHAPTER TWO

"Mom, why do I have to leave my cell phone behind? How am I supposed to talk to friends?" Phoebe whined. The seventeen-year-old had come into her full powers and thought this gave her rights to make decisions for the family.

Phoebe was more like a secretary bird than a sparrow. Her hair formed a halo around her head and she was forever looking online for ways to control or style it. Her younger siblings laughed at her as she stood in front of the mirror and encouraged her silky curls into strange and amazing creations. If she heard their giggles she was quick to scowl, but not for long, chasing them through the forests with her long legs and enviable agility. Her large green and hazel eyes would crinkle with laughter as she pretended to be angry with the younger children.

As the most popular girl in school, Phoebe had love-struck boys chasing after her who in turn were chased off by an irritated Alpheus. Every girl in school wanted to be her friend and she never missed a party or an outing with her friends. She always kept herself aloof from their dramas. There was really no one she felt close to, sometimes preferring to be with her family, much to the astonishment of her school friends.

"Sorry, Phoebe, no such luck. We're on the run. Now go collect clothing, bedding and some baskets to put what food we can find. The honey will be good. Hurry, hurry my girl. I do love you and know you find this hard, but listen to me. It's not only for your own good, but for the safety of our whole family." Nyoni said to soothe her angry daughter.

Phoebe rolled her eyes but did as asked and gathered food in baskets and warm clothing for cool nights on the road. A text message came in from a friend and she became distracted for a moment, but soon got back to her chores and sang a tune as she strapped the baskets to the sides of a large bull.

Phoebe stroked the bull gently as it shifted at his unexpected burden. "Shh, silly creature. You're strong and able to carry such a light load with ease."

Her singing soothed the animal. Phoebe then chased after her younger siblings. She strapped a two-year-old to her back and took the hand of her four-year-old brother. They loved their big sister and tagged along as long as she sang to them in her sweet voice.

Alpheus nursed his wound and winced at every movement he made, as he contemplated ways to keep his cows. The vultures gathered around the dead bull and he did not want them to feast on his other cattle. The women wiped out their tracks with a sharp wind when they herded the cattle into a high pasture within the forest.

In the treetops Sarah kept an eye out for the soldiers roaming the countryside and let out a shrill whistle as she caught sight of the enemy. Sipho, the twelve-year-old son of Thandi, grabbed a whip and with a whistle of his own had the dogs yapping at the heels of the cattle as he ushered them into the protection of the tree line.

"Good boy, Sipho." Alpheus hurried after them. The younger children were still in the cave where they were hidden and it was now a race to get the rest of the family to safety.

The women flew up in the trees and surveyed the road ahead. Sarah hid their trail, but there were tell-tale signs a good tracker could follow. The broken and bent pieces of grass where a cow or bull had bumped into it, a stone rolled out of place exposing a different coloured earth beneath and lichen rubbed off the side of a tree along the path.

Thandi came alongside Sarah and they created a rain storm to hide what they could. Wind whipped through the branches so broken leaves and lichen would be attributed to the storm. It was all they could do.

They watched for many hours as the soldiers searched the kraal. At sunset, the men set the huts alight and then camped there overnight. The glow of their burning homes could be seen by the sentries. At sunrise, the soldiers marched towards the town and Thandi noticed one of the men talking on his cell phone and then looking at the tree tops in search of signs of them.

Alpheus had needed stitches to close the wound properly. Nyoni's neat stitches were as good as any surgeon could wish for. Sarah made him herbal tea to dull the pain. Using the bark of a Willow tree she gave him a piece to chew on when the pain returned.

The children were fed with the meagre stores they were carrying. All the adults knew it would not last. With the cattle in tow it was almost impossible to use the air to travel, plus they worried if they flew above the treeline, they would be visible to ground troops. A pannier system was rigged up for the cows to carry the supplies and the youngest baby. Everyone else was expected to walk and while they were walking they were to look for food in the form of fruit or edible bugs.

The first night on the trail Alpheus managed to snare three rabbits for their meal. Alpheus and Sipho dug a pit and laid the fire in the bottom and then used branches to diffuse the smoke. The smell was the only thing giving them away and it was considered a risk they were prepared to take to be able to eat something hot and nourishing.

When the sun set the women took turns to stand guard through the night. Alpheus and Sipho were in charge of the children in the cave and Nyoni took Phoebe with her to sleep in the trees above the path. Phoebe still complained about the loss of her home and friends, but was much too tired to talk for long.

"Mom, I love my home. I've only recently been given my own room and I really was so excited, but now I don't know what my future holds and I'm scared it'll mean us living in caves and keeping guard in trees for the rest of our lives." She realised she was whining as she added. "Sorry if I sound grumpy but I wish this had never happened. Wake me if you need me in the night. I'll sleep for a while and then I'll take over so you can sleep to. Love you Mom, to the moon and back and throughout all eternity."

Nyoni smiled as she watched her daughter settle down in the leaves and covered her with a soft cloth to protect her from the dew.

"I love you much more. More than you can ever imagine. I would've been happier if none of this had happened, but it's too late now to cry over spilt milk. Sleep well, my girl."

They were woken by a dull thunder surrounding them on all sides. Trees shivered in the early morning mist as if in terror. Black greasy clouds approached in the distance. Nyoni turned into an eagle and flew up in the sky to see what came into their pristine wilderness. Her heart quailed at what she saw.

The devastation of large behemoths devouring the forest below brought a tear to her eye and she had to remind herself what these men destroyed could be repaired with plenty of care. It might take a while, but it could be done. Alpheus would hate the destruction, but he would be the first to get his hands dirty in the restoration of his beloved land.

Trucks and troop carriers made their way slowly across the fields churning up the crops in their way. Soldiers took pot shots at the corn cobs and wild chickens scuttled for cover in amongst the underbrush. The army were stopped by the dense forest, but the crushing of the forest would solve that issue with time.

The women returned to the family and Alpheus who waited for them with a grin on his face.

"I know how we can get around the troops. Sipho and I've been looking at the map and we know where to go." He put his arm around his son's shoulders and beamed at his wives.

Alpheus laid Raz's map on the floor inside the cave and they all looked at it with interest. He marked out where the other Air Whisperer kraals could be found. They worried if it was a good idea to bring their problems on to the heads of innocent people. People as persecuted as they were. There was another sign on the map intriguing Alpheus when he looked at it. Now he pointed it out to the others.

"What does this look like? To me it's an elephant. Surely elephants offer protection and strength. We need both in abundance at the moment?"

Having no real choice but to seek out someone strong enough to look for them, they planned to follow the map towards the symbol. They hoped whoever was there would take pity on them and give them sanctuary.

"This is a cave system linking our position with the Elephant people over here." He pointed to the map.

"My dear husband, this is the same map the soldiers will use. Won't they know about this system?" Sarah's voice was worried.

"We can hide the entry point with a few boulders. Even if it doesn't stop them, at least it'll slow them down." He pointed to Nyoni. "You could get a storm to wash the soil and rocks across the entrance to the caves and the soldiers will never know how to get in."

With a plan they moved with purpose. Alpheus set up the cattle with panniers of large baskets hanging over their backs to hold all their goods. The children drunk their full of fresh milk and he handed a calabash to each of the wives with some of the creamy liquid. It might not have been a true breakfast, but it was enough to fill their stomachs.

Sipho and Phoebe were sent to loosen rocks from the hillside above. Dogs herded the cattle into the dark interior. The cows were not pleased with their new abode. Alpheus took a lead-rope looped around the oldest bull and cajoled and crooned. He encouraged them to follow him down the passage.

The women observed the soldiers as they marched closer to their position. At lunchtime Nyoni conjured up the storm her husband had asked for. Holding her hand out in front of her, she directed the rain to the loosened rocks and soil. As soon as it moved she changed into a bat and flew through the cave entrance. The rocks crashed down, cutting off the light. She met up with her family as they trudged through the dark.

They had not stopped for food, eating fruit as they walked. Alpheus chewed on the bark of the white willow tree and his face was grey and gaunt from the pain of his wound. Sarah and Thandi walked up and down the group, helping where they could. Sipho took the rope from his father and led the bull along the narrow passage. Sometimes the roof dipped so low it scraped along the backs of the cattle and the adults were forced to walk bent over.

The air was stale and it took all of Nyoni's patience to calm the anxieties of her children. Phoebe asked if they were nearly at their destination and Nyoni felt like screaming at her to shut up. What made it worse was Thandi had flown back down the tunnel and had reported the troops were almost through the barricade.

"How on earth did they find us so quickly? We were so careful to cover our tracks. What did we do wrong?" Whispered Sarah.

They reached a large cave and even though the air was dank. They rested for a few hours to regain their strength. All the women needed fresh air to be able to use their powers to the best of their abilities, but what air they had would have to do for now. Sipho and Thandi went back down the cave system and tried to create barriers to slow the soldiers down to allow the family to escape.

They returned dusty, tired and thirsty. Alpheus found a small spring in the corner of the cave and they were able to drink some water. The cows were milked and the children fed on bowls of milk mixed with putu porridge.

As Sipho sipped this concoction he glanced up and noticed Phoebe hiding behind some rocks. Her face lit up with a strange light and Sipho knew how the soldiers were able to track them.

"Mom, Mom." He called softly. Thandi came up to him, wearily and he nodded towards his sister using her cell phone. "I think it's how the soldiers found us, Mom. They tracked Phoebe's phone."

Thandi looked over at Nyoni and beckoned her over and explained to her what they had seen. Changing into a large bat, Nyoni flew straight at her daughter. Landing on her head, she screeched in a high-pitched scream. "The phone, silly child. The soldiers are following your signal. You've endangered your whole family because of a stupid need to talk to friends. Give it here."

Phoebe looked up in shock and her mother was able to grab the phone out of her hand. A disjointed voice came from the phone asking Phoebe what she was wearing to a party in Melmoth.

Phoebe had eyes the size of saucers as she waited for her mother's wrath to descend. Nyoni looked at the small device in her hand and was tempted to dash the phone to shreds on the rocks. Sweat gathered on her forehead as she battled to contain her distress. A tear formed in her eye and she clenched her teeth as she bit back words she might regret.

Her anger was more about their whole situation and the cell phone had been the catalyst for her fury. Nyoni took a deep breath and with a bit of effort she was able to bring things back into focus.

Alpheus observed the exchange and held up his hand to get their attention.

"We can use it to lead them away." He explained his plan and calmed the feelings of his wives and daughter. Ever the strategist, he already understood the significance of the troops tracking them so accurately.

"We can use the phone and its signal to get them lost inside the mountain. There are lots of little caves appearing to go somewhere, but really only going deeper into the rock. This is not a bad thing, it might've been a silly thing to do, but it's not the end of the world. We need a few hours head start to get to safety. We can do it. We're almost there. Their technology won't help the soldiers if we're clever."

He closed his hand over Nyoni's and the phone.

"Take this and fly down the caves until you find a dead end. Place this phone deep inside and hopefully it will lead our pursuers astray." He knew they would need every second they could find to outrun the battle fit soldiers. He looked at the younger children and worried for their future. He loved all of his ten children but his first responsibility was the weakest and smallest amongst them. He hoped his elder children would find a way to escape.

Nyoni said, "I saw the perfect place." Flying back towards where they had come from, she found a narrow channel through to a large cave with a deep pond in the one corner. She placed the phone carefully on a rock shelf and then returned to the family.

"We need to carry on. Phoebe, you'll lead the way and no dragging your feet. Do you understand?" Nyoni glared at her significantly.

Phoebe answered sufficiently chastised. "Yes Mom. Sorry, I didn't think talking to my friends would be wrong."

CHAPTER THREE

The weary travellers shuffled on through the night. Sleeping children were draped over the backs of long suffering cattle and the achingly tired parents walked in a trance. As dawn rose they came to the exit of the caves.

No longer were there forests to the edge of the horizon, now there were fields of grasslands with thorn trees dotted around. They could glimpse a distant river glittering in the sun. Herds of antelope grazed. Zebra and giraffe added their distinctive patterns to the landscape.

Alpheus looked for somewhere safe to rest and couldn't find respite anywhere at all. He looked back at the mountainside and saw baboons romping through the rocks. Hyrax and monkeys peered around outcrops and he knew he should be able to find food to feed his hungry hoard, but no hiding place for them. No small forest, no deep ravines.

Alpheus sat down and put his head in his hands as he contemplated the future. All their frantic efforts were doomed to failure.

The cows needed milking again and Phoebe and Sipho silently took their places next to the beasts and milked. Nyoni fed the children and Thandi and Sarah took to the skies in search of help.

Once the children were fed Nyoni flew back into the caves to see where their pursuers had got to. She found them asleep in the cave where the family had rested. Their ruse had not worked as they had hoped, but at least it had slowed the enemy down.

Thandi found a ravine to hide. It was not ideal and if the soldiers came too close they were bound to find them, but it was all they had for the moment. The family stumbled down the hillside and into their hiding place. Children fell asleep where they landed and it took all of Alpheus's reserves of strength to hide the agony he was in as he secured the cattle to clumps of grass and low-lying scrub.

Sarah hid their tracks with her Air Whisperer powers. All they could do was hope for the best.

Sipho and Phoebe took their turn as sentries. Their eyes focused on the entrance of the cave. About lunch time they saw movement.

They watched as the soldiers came out of the cave and consulted their gadgets. A flying drone was dispatched to search them out. The family hid under the cover of grasses and bushes. Thandi tightened her grip on her crossbow. Prepared to shoot the drone out of the sky. But it would still reveal their location.

As the drone flew closer to them, a lone horseman appeared in the distance.

He had shining gold hair and skin as brown as a berry. The drone buzzed around his head as he made his way closer to them. The family held their breath afraid to see what would happen with this new development. He drew level with the soldiers as they marched. "What is your business here, Zulu soldiers?" Thandi took on the body of a Shrike and flew close enough to observe their encounter.

"We're here on the King's command, searching out dissidents who have fled from their duty."

"Dissidents?" He said in a booming voice. "What are these criminals doing on my lands? I am Ndlovu and I am the protector of these lands. Surely they wouldn't be foolish enough to venture into my domain?" As he queried the soldier he looked directly at Thandi as if he could perceive her real form.

A family of elephants materialised from the veldt. The soldiers, scared of these large pachyderms, stood closer together for protection. The matriarch of the elephants came up to the horseman and draped her trunk across the horseman's shoulders.

The Corporal fidgeted with his rifle and the horseman shook his head and tsked at the man.

"Don't be stupid, my dear fellow. The gun is like a pea shooter against an elephant. You'll make her mad at you and she'd stomp you into the ground in a heartbeat. Now put the pop gun down and leave this land." Ndlovu commanded them.

"We can't leave sir, we've a job to do. We have to find these people or else the king will hold us accountable and the consequences wouldn't be good." The Corporal was very nervous and continually glanced around him at his fellow soldiers as if for support.

"Oh, you don't need to concern yourselves with nonsense. All you have to do is travel North for a day and you'll be in Swaziland and have freedom."

The soldiers looked at him as if he was mad and shook their heads in unison like a row of bobble heads, the Corporal spoke for them all as he replied, "Unacceptable. Our place is with our king and not to run and hide like cowards. We'll take the consequences of our actions like loyal servants, no matter what they are."

The elephants crowded closer and the horseman was now within striking distance of the closest soldier. The largest elephant wrapped her trunk around the Corporal's leg and yanked him into the air effortlessly. The Corporal flailed helplessly before the elephant returned him to the ground. Pale and shaking he gathered his uselessly gun.

"Go now," Ndlovu whispered quietly, "and don't return, ever."

For all their bluster, the soldiers did not argue, but looked to their Corporal for guidance. The horseman pointed his finger at the mountain they had recently exited. They all turned to look and none uttered a word as they retraced their steps.

The horseman watched them until the last soldier entered the cave. He turned towards Nyoni and beckoned her closer. She flittered to the ground in front of him and metamorphosed back into her human form.

"Welcome to our home of the elephant people. Call your people and we'll take you somewhere you can rest." He watched as Alpheus' family rose from the shallow gully and pulling their cattle forward, they advanced towards the pachyderms.

Alpheus bowed low. "We're the Air Whisperers. Fugitives from the Zulu king and seek sanctuary with the people of the Plains. We wish no harm and we come in peace and beg your indulgence for but a few days so we can make plans."

The horseman bowed in his saddle and declared in a booming voice. "I'm Ndlovu and you're welcome to our home. We're pleased to greet you and your family."

The home of the elephants was not far away and Alpheus was surprised he had not noticed it from the mountainside. It was a fortress made from sandstone with great carvings of elephants at the gates. The gates were flung wide so the elephants could easily enter at will. Made from the trunks of the Fever trees, they were woven together with broad bands of embossed copper with strange symbols.

Antelope grazed the grasslands around the edges and large Secretary birds patrolled the ramparts.

As the elephants walked through the gate the pachyderms shrunk down and changed into men and women. Their noses were longer than anyone Alpheus had ever seen before. Their ears stood out from their heads and turned at each little sound in an interesting and strange way.

Many of them had egret birds perched on their shoulders and Ndlovu was the only golden-haired person amongst them. The other elephants had changed into a variety of wild haired humans of different hues. A blue haired man with a scar running across his face smiled at the family and welcomed a bevy of children all eager for a climb over his broad back.

A red-haired woman approached them. "Good morning, my name is Izzie and I'm thrilled to welcome you to our humble home. Come and sit while my family brings you some food." She ushered them to comfortable chairs woven from some of the Fever tree branches and covered in the softest animal fur imaginable.

Nyoni thanked her and gratefully sank down into the comfort. The gates closed behind them and the ramparts were manned by not only the Secretary birds, but also by meerkats with catapults strapped to their waists.

Phoebe fascinated with this strange new world had to be invited more than once to take a seat. With the children gathered around their feet, their cattle safely contained in a boma made from the branches of thorn trees, the family allowed the ache of tiredness to descend on them.

The stress and worry of the past few days took its toll and Sarah burst into tears. She hid her face in Nyoni's shoulder as Sarah sobbed. No one said anything to her and let her have her moment of weakness.

Phoebe and Sipho found children their own age and shyly became acquainted by comparing favourite singers and complaining about the fact they were limited as to their ability to shape shift until they were young adults. It felt good to speak to other teenagers who had similar challenges to themselves.

"How do you cope with the rules your parents set? I mean there are always one thousand questions before I can go out. Don't they trust me?" Complained Phoebe.

"Oh yeah, Phoebe, but remember the time you snuck out wearing a really revealing outfit and Mom saw photos online and freaked out?" Sipho laughed as his sister looked shamefaced.

"Oh, okay, I know I'm not always perfect like you, my little brother, but the party was amazing and worth the two-week grounding."

"I did something similar a year ago and Mom and Dad still bring it up each time I ask to go out. But what I hate is they have banned me from changing shape outside of the confines of the family. They say it'll freak people out. Do they think I'm silly enough to do it in front of strangers? Surely my friends would be okay with it? It would mean I could get to places in half the time and even take a few friends on my back for a ride."

The other children all agreed they hated strictures on revealing themselves. They heard their parents calling them to dinner and conversation ceased as they attended to their hunger.

Izzie and some of the other family members brought plates of delicious fruits and nuts. Ndlovu bowed his head over the food and asked a blessing to nourish their bodies and to keep them safe from danger or harm. Great casks of spring water were brought for the guests.

After they ate their fill Alpheus and Ndlovu went off to speak privately.

Alpheus said, "I'm sorry we had to bring this problem to your door step."

Ndlovu snorted. "This is not just your problem. Do you truly think the Zulu king would spare us? When they finish beating the Air Whisperers into the ground they will turn to new warriors and our people will be top of the list. We are protecting ourselves by choosing the battle field now."

Alpheus still felt guilty but he didn't contradict Ndlovu. The Zulu were insatiable and Ndlovu's people weren't safe.

The women and children went to a large lake for a good bath. They were able to change into clean clothes for the first time in three days and everyone felt much better by the end of it. The hosts found games for the little ones to play and the children found a reservoir of energy the adults could only envy. Some of the elephants changed from human to animal and the children were able to ride on their backs.

Phoebe showed off her Air Whisperer skills by tumbling through the air, barely touching the surface of the water with her toes as she pirouetted and twirled while a beautiful bird song rang out from her throat. Sipho slid down the trunk of a large elephant. As he was about to dive into the water the elephant grabbed him by the ankle and threw him high in the air, much to the delight of the younger children.

The two men stayed secluded for the whole afternoon and it was only as the sun set and great pans of food were simmering on the fire, they came back. Alpheus rolled up his map and Ndlovu rested his hand on Alpheus' shoulder in a symbol of unity.

Once all the children were fed they were put to bed in hammocks around the courtyard and covered with gossamer mosquito netting, the adults could sit and discuss their options.

Alpheus laid out the map and everyone leaned in closer. He picked up a stick and pointed at the symbol of the elephants on the map. "This is where we're now. As you can see, we're surrounded by mountains with only a few protected paths into this region. This is good in one way, but bad in another. It means this kingdom can be protected with minimal troops, but if we try to leave it'll be easy for the soldiers to guard the area and catch us with ease. Here is where we came in and these here are the exits." He stood back. "We can't stay here for ever. It isn't ideal, but we can stay here and prepare ourselves. Train our family to defend themselves. But at the end of the day, we have to leave and face the consequences of our choices."

No one offered a word while the firelight flickered on their worried faces. There was no hope of them ever returning to their old life or a better future regardless of what they did.

They each went off to bed with their minds filled with ideas to be mulled over. Alpheus chose to sleep with Sarah at night because she was the one most scared of their future. He kissed each of his children and then his two other wives were given a hug and a kiss, before he gathered a large Swazi karosse and wrapped it around Sarah and himself.

Nyoni and Thandi huddled together and spoke for a while until they could not stay awake a moment more.

"Are you scared?" Nyoni asked Thandi.

Thandi snorted and said, "We're safe here."

There was a long silence between them before Nyoni added, "I'd be fine as long as the children were safe."

CHAPTER FOUR

They woke to the shrill scream of a meerkat. "Krirr, krirr, krirr."

Izzie translated the alarm for her guests.

"The Zulu airships are at the mountains. The meerkats say the enemy will be here in about half an hour. We have time to get the children out of harm's way. The meerkats and monkeys will do what they can to help, but they are not strong enough to cause much damage. They will communicate via translators. Our engineers are working on a portable translator, but it's not quite finished."

Air ships bristling with guns crested the mountain ridges. Ndlovu and Izzie marshalled the children into safety inside the walls of the fortress. Elephants were being dressed in suits of bullet proof jackets by an army of animals. Izzie changed into a large pachyderm with bronze and copper armour. Ndlovu jumped onto her back and raised his voice so his words reached each corner of the courtyard with ease.

"Today our homeland is being invaded by evil people. We will win the day. This is our home and no one is taking it from us." Ndlovu called as he changed into his elephant persona.

Alpheus stood on the ramparts with his fighting stick at hand. His three wives and daughter were ready to do battle in protection of their children. Sarah had a quiver of arrows on her back and Thandi had her crossbow ready.

Nyoni called the birds of the air to help. High in the sky, eagles and hawks circled and lower down the smaller birds sat patiently on branches and amongst the grasses.

Phoebe waited for the fighting to start with a tinge of trepidation in her heart. Excitement quivered in every pore of her being. She could see the glint of sunshine off the armaments. Soldiers stepped to the railings and she could clearly see assault rifles and high-powered guns pointed straight at them. She could fight these men who were much larger than herself, but how it could be achieved had her calculating angles and trajectories, velocity and impact. Who knew mathematics could be so helpful in a war situation?

Nyoni looked over at her daughter and called out. "Aim for their limbs where the damage will be affective in disabling them, as well as tying up the medical contingent. We want them to scream loudly to distract others. You can do it, Phoebe."

Phoebe smiled at her mother and checked her own weapons one last time.

The battle ensued with the first volley coming from the air ships. Huge flaming balls of burning tar rained down into the courtyard. This was the signal they had all been waiting for and with a trumpet of her trunk, Izzie led the charge out of the fortress. The air ships were much too high to be affected by the elephants themselves, but the pachyderms raised their trunks and sent forth a sound, shaking the air.

The air ships wobbled in the sky and soldiers were thrown around from side to side as the shock waves hit them. The Air Whisperers materialised amongst the soldiers and created havoc with their arrows and crossbows as they sliced through the ranks.

Nyoni arrived with her flotilla of feathered friends and bombarded them with sharp claws and vicious stabs of the beaks into vulnerable places on the body. Nyoni took the shape of a large raptor and swooped out of the sky like an avenging angel.

Many of the soldiers had no protection at all. They were under the mistaken idea their height in the air would be their ally and not their downfall. Small sparrows and white-eyes flew in the face of the men and blinded them as Nyoni stepped up behind them and using her stabbing spear, ended their lives.

Many soldiers jumped out of the air ships as they tried to escape the attack. Some of the commanders were better prepared with extensive armour and weaponry.

Thandi was wounded with an assegai and had lost plenty of blood, so retreated while she could still do so. Changing into particles she floated down to the ground where Alpheus was ready to tend her wounds. He kissed her softly on the head. "Relax, Sweetheart. No need to worry. Your wound is barely a little scratch." He used disinfectant to clean the wound and bandaged it to protect the wound from further injury.

Thandi grinned as she rushed back into the fray. As she approached the fortress a meerkat was struck by an enemy missile and fell out off the wall. Thandi reached up and caught the furry little body. She rushed the injured soldier back to Alpheus before once again joining the fight.

Ndlovu and Izzie called over to Tembe, "Tembe, come climb on our backs. We'll try and grab their rudders and shake them up a bit. They won't be expecting an elephant to reach into the sky and we can catch them off guard."

Ndlovu changed into his very impressive elephantine shape, Izzie ran up his rump and landed on his back, changing herself into an elephant. Finally Tembe clambered over her parents' backs. She stood tall on Izzie's back before she changed into her animal form. Ndlovu grunted, "Girls you need to cut back on the nuts." But he held his ground.

Positioned underneath an airship Tembe was able to grab the rudder. With a twist of her trunk and rip it from its moorings. The airship spun out of control. As it crashed into the thorn tree forest, the three pachyderms let out a yell of victory. The airships rose higher in the air to avoid them.

Phoebe had the strength and speed of youth and was everywhere, jumping from air ship to air ship as she saw a need.

She plucked arrows from the air aimed at friends and family. Using her short stabbing spear to injure and distract where she could. She laughed gleefully as she pulled out the pins holding the rudder of the airships in place. As she leant down to disconnect a fan belt, a large Zulu warrior bore down on her with a knobkerrie raised high above his head in a death strike.

Phoebe saw his reflection in the shiny cover of the pistons and whirled around in time to duck below the swinging stick. Outweighed by many kilograms she relied on her understanding of physics and how to manipulate mass. As he lunged once more to attack her, she sidestepped neatly and his weight and momentum propelled him over the side of the airship and into oblivion. With arms flailing and lungs screaming in terror, the soldier met his doom amongst the mighty elephant army below.

Phoebe peered down at the poor unfortunate man and for a second felt a little bit of remorse.

Sarah stayed on the ground to fire her arrows and packed them with tar and set them alight before shooting them into the ships. Usually Sarah was the passive wife in the group and found it difficult to be the aggressor, but when her children and family were under threat she soon forgot her aversion to violence. Crying a few quiet tears Sarah saw the devastation her arrows caused. A silent prayer was uttered that she would be forgiven her actions before she drew back her arrows once more.

The fiery missiles were deadly accurate and many soldiers felt the impact of the flames. Every little bit of distraction helped the cause of the defenders and Sarah was able to accept what she was doing was necessary.

Ndlovu and his troops collected up the fallen soldiers. Airmen who fell from the airships were crushed under the massive feet of the elephants. Izzie trumpeted orders to her people. Even the youngest elephant had a job to do and helped the animal soldiers on the battlements.

New ammunition was brought to the beleaguered troops. They rushed bowls of water to the thirsty and food to the hungry. Small meerkat paws were raised to grasp the water calabashes and gently pat a hand in thankfulness. Large elephants halted their violence as the children approached and enemies were held still under massive feet while the Ndlovu people drank long and gratefully from the proffered nourishment.

Small fires started in three of the air ships and they retreated to the mountains in defeat, but the more heavily armoured ships had a devastating effect on the courtyard. Their flaming tar balls splashed up the sides of the fortress and scorched ugly scars close to where the smallest children hid.

The elephants were kept busy collecting water from the lake and putting out fires where they could. The tar balls were smothered with buckets of sand.

The older children, under the guidance of Sipho, joined together to lug barrels of sand to the worst affected areas. The younger children used spades to scoop the sand over the flames. Many had tear streaks down their faces yet they never faltered in their efforts to save what they could.

The battle continued all day and the defenders managed to grab a short drink here and there, but not much in the way of respite. The younger meerkats and monkeys kept busy running messages and ushered injured birds into the sanctuary within the walls. An elderly meerkat sat quietly in a corner offering hugs to those needing comfort amongst the children.

When they thought the day was over and they could relax a little bit, the ground troops arrived. Marching through the mountain passes and bringing with them cannons and great contraptions of destruction. Defeat darkened their minds. They could not fight alone against the masses of soldiers heading their way.

Alpheus asked, "Is this us?"

Ndlovu shook his head, "We aren't defeated yet, my new friend." Ndlovu called out a mighty roar. A wordless cry to all the creatures to join their battle.

All the animals within the sound of his voice stopped what they were doing to consider their options. To join or to abstain. How would a battle between the Zulu and the Ndlovu affect them? Was it worth their while to become involved?

The lion obliged because of the thought of all the free meals he could get from the fallen soldiers. The cheetah was keen to act in the dark of the night as a stealth attacker and even the baboons sharpened their teeth in anticipation of a good fight. The warthog decided there was nothing to be gained and declined the invite, the zebra and giraffe did not see how their skills could help and thought they might hinder the efforts and took refuge as far as they could from the violence. The rhino did not enjoy working with others and preferred to keep his own company. None the less he sharpened his horn in case he would be needed. The hippo and crocodile were too far away to be of any use and sent a message of support back to Ndlovu.

Many of the monkeys and meerkats showed signs of exhaustion and all of them bore the scars of war and had wounds needing attention. As a chieftain Ndlovu had to make sure his troops were cared for and if it required the blood lust of the carnivores, then so be it.

CHAPTER FIVE

Ndlovu and Alpheus stood on the ramparts of the fortress to survey the advancing troops. With a call shaking the earth and the air, Ndlovu let forth the dogs, or in this case the lions of war. They picked off unwary soldiers on the periphery of the marchers. As soon as the commanders realised what was happening they tightened up the ranks.

The snakes rose out of the holes in the veldt and bit exposed limbs. Baboons jumped off rocks and sunk savage teeth into tender skin, lions attacked in packs and cheetahs dragged screaming enemy soldiers into trees to feast at their leisure.

The soldiers stepped over their companions and advanced relentlessly towards the defenders. They started a chant and with each tenth step they would hit their shields with their guns.

"Bulala, bulala, bulala, Ndlovu." Banged on the shields and then, "Bulala, bulala, bulala, Ndlovu." It was intimidating to say the least and raised the hair on the backs of many of the observers.

The moon and the stars lit the sky as the troops continued. Food and drink was given to all within the fortress and wounds were tended to as they took it in turns to care for each other. Exhausted troops took naps as they trusted their allies to continue the assault and keep the enemies at bay. Screams and the odd chatter of gunfire split the night air.

Nyoni changed into an owl and patrolled. Thandi took to the air and looked for any advantage to be found. Phoebe silently danced on the air and did what damage she could on the hovering airships. Their strong searchlights was the scourge of the defenders. Their destruction was their primary target. Thandi stood guard as Phoebe worked her engineering magic.

Nyoni called out a warning when soldiers patrolled close to the two women. Phoebe went back to earth and helped Sarah as she could do no more damage on the airships without being injured herself. Phoebe had two wounds, but were not serious. Light headed from all the fighting as she had not eaten or drunk for many hours Phoebe was pleased to have a break from the battle itself.

Nyoni brought down a low mist to disorientate the attackers. Sarah and Phoebe looked after the little ones and made sure they were not getting too stressed. Phoebe told stories of great bravery and then made up songs of humour to sing of the cowardice of the Zulu.

She whispered, "Auntie Mary hid herself down a well during the Bambatha rebellion as assegai wielding thugs ransacked the homestead." The children gasped at the image Phoebe created. Easy with the Zulu warriors so close by with their own weapons and menace.

"Auntie Mary heard the men crashing through the bushes as they approached the house. As she put on her shoes, she could hear the men in the kitchen smashing cupboards as they looked for alcohol and she raced down the passage towards the children who lay fast asleep in their beds. Pushing them out the windows, she then went back to wake the mothers and helped them to escape."

Phoebe picked up one of the children and the squealed in delight as Phoebe demonstrated how Aunty Mary helped the children to escape.

"'Let's go quietly children, we need to hide from the bad bad men.' But where to hide that the men would not discover them? The barn was not good, the forest was too exposed and then Auntie Mary remembered the old well, with its ancient rope and rusted buckets. The bottom of the well was dry as a bone and no one had used it for many years. But it would be a tight fit." Phoebe pulled the children close as she showed the dimensions of the well and how tight the children would have been with Aunty Mary. The warmth of the children was comforting to Phoebe even though the intent was to ease the children's fears.

"She gathered the children and their mothers together and told them of her idea. The gunfire was getting closer all the time and no one wanted to stay in the open. Mothers agreed that it was the only option. So, four mothers, ten children and Auntie Mary quickly lifted the lid of the well and Susannah, the strongest woman went down first. Then Mary helped them all one by one to descend. She did three trips with children on her back when they were too big or heavy for the bucket. It was a tight fit at the bottom of the well and very dark, but it was safe and dry." Phoebe grabbed one of the other children and humped them on her back and pretended to climb down the well as they clung to her back like a baby monkey.

"No one had brought food or drink with them and the children were soon complaining about being hungry. Auntie Mary gave the children a pebble to suck and told them to imagine it was a juicy piece of fruit, but to make sure that they did not swallow it because then they would never be able to go swimming again!" Phoebe dug in a pocket and pulled out some lint covered mints. She handed them out to the children for them to suck on.

"Dawn came and so did the bandits. They peered down the well and the family were sure they would be discovered, but it was so dark and deep that they stayed hidden and hugged each other for comfort. The sun rose higher and each minute seemed like forever. Some managed to sleep and the children snuggled into the warmth of the adults and dozed off for a moment's peace. The sun started to set on the day and it was now time to make their move if they were to survive."

Phoebe picked up the second youngest of the children. Barely one they were still wobbly on their feet. She cuddled the child close who wiggled out of her arms. Making the other children laugh as Phoebe continued with the story.

"Mary rocked a sick baby for hours while the mother soothed the scared little ones. Auntie Mary of short stature. Auntie Mary of shaking hands and scared of the dark." Phoebe shook in mock fear to demonstrate Mary's actions.

"But Auntie Mary became fearless when she saw the small ones threatened. Auntie Mary climbed up out of the well in the dark of the night, climbed the ancient rope hand over hand till blisters covered her palms." Again, Phoebe acted out Mary's bravery and climbed an invisible rope.

"At any moment the bandits could find them. As Auntie Mary lifted her chin above the edge, she expected someone to yell, but no one did. A drunk man lay snoring nearby and she shivered in dread. But the children were hungry and there was no going back now. There was food to find, bandits to avoid and a safe haven to find. Auntie Mary climbed back down and put the first child on her back."

Her hands held up to her chin so it looked like she was peering over the top of the well.

"'Hold tight.' She whispered and turned back to the old rope that stretched up above her. She spat on her palms and took a deep breath as she prepared herself for her mammoth task." Phoebe made a snort as she pretended to spit into her hands.

"She raised each baby up bucket by bucket and then walked for hours carrying three children at a time through the dangerous wilderness. The mothers encouraged their little ones along the dark path, Mary encouraged the mothers and she herself bit her cheek to stop herself from crying in fear. She heard strange noises and tried to peer into the shadows." The children took the signal in the story and started to climb over Phoebe who grunted in effort as the children were getting older and heavier than when she had first started telling this story to the children years ago. She let them clamber for a moment before she set them all back onto the ground. She made a shushing sound with her finger to her lips and started looking around and under everything near them.

"She never knew in the dark of the night a predator was stalking them. Silently, stealthily, hiding in every bit of darkness. The slinky predator walked with feet avoiding every stick or stone. Trying not to make a noise and give away his plan."

Phoebe pretended to be a vicious leopard and grabbed one of the children and picked her up to the enjoyment of the other children.

"Until finally within sight of safety and when the family thought they were safe, he sprang and snapped his wicked teeth firmly around a tender tasty morsel of human flesh." Phoebe gave the child a pretend bite on her foot and tickled her little sister until she giggled aloud.

"A sharp cry of pain and everyone stopped in their tracks. Mary grabbed a stick to fight off the leopard attacking them and who was now carrying a screaming child off into the dark. She hit it over the head so hard it dropped the child and wobbled off into the night with a sore head and an even more bruised ego. Whimpering quietly to itself in disgust."

Phoebe set down the child on her knee as Phoebe finally took a seat. "And the child, was our Dad. Yes, if you look at your Father's ankle you can still see the marks left by the teeth of the leopard. The stick your Dad carries is fashioned from the stick used by his Auntie Mary all those years ago. And no one ever called her Scaredy Mary ever again."

Phoebe pulled up her own skirt to show off her ankle as if the marks on her dad's ankle would magically be on her own.

"This was the song she taught us and I'll now sing it for you, with a few bits added by myself." Holding her hands in front of her like an opera singer she sang in a gruff voice.

"The Bambatha rebellion raged and raged
   With screams and yells and all sorts of stuff
   Children and babies, Mary and women climbed
   And clambered down the old family well.
   Slither, slip, slippedy slip they went.
   Quietly quietly they sat in the dark.
   The men went looking for help and still they sat.

   The sounds of fighting came closer and closer
   Knees shook and teeth chattered in fear.
   Boom bang the gun fired above
   Until at last, the silence of night descended
   Quietly, silently they climbed out the well,
   Hand over hand, babies on backs.
   Grunt and groan they climbed, climbed, climbed.
   Hands aching, knees shivering, shiver, shiver.

   Men with guns were really scary,
   But something else was lurking with eyes on
   The juicy little children. Yum, yum, yum,
   A thing scarier than guns, something with teeth
   Something that moved so, so quietly
   Closer he came and closer still
   The beast could almost taste the child
   Yum yummity yum almost mine, he thought

The night was dim dimmity dim,
When whoosh whoosh the stick hit whack whack
Flying through the dark the leopard leapt
Who was this who dared attack
Why it was Auntie Scaredy Mary
Whack twack the stick hit
Twackedy whack a smack.
Twackety smack a back.
Scaredy leopard brave Auntie Mary.

The family stumbled into a village at last
Safe, safe from danger and fear.
No more, nasty cruel Bambatha
No more leopards or dark night
Warm beds for all. Cuddle cuddle cuddle
Snore grunt and grunt in sleep
Smiles and happy thoughts all night long.
In the light of day home again, home again.

The soldiers came and burned our house
When twackety smack Dad whacked clack
Raz cried and cried as the stick hit
Whackety thwack the Zulu soldiers ran
Mom hit one, Dad hit another
Not scared at all, brave brave
Air whisperers all.
Whackedy smack a twack.
Smackedy twack a smack."

Phoebe smiled at her siblings. "The Bambatha rebellion did not last long and the bad men were punished. The leopard found a juicy rabbit to fill its tummy and never looked at another child again. We can be brave like Auntie Mary and not worry about bad men or even hungry leopards. Now it is time to sleep little ones. Night, night."

The children loved it and were soon lulled into a sense of security and were able to fall asleep with peace. The old meerkat dispensed hugs to those in need and was joined by a senior monkey who had retired from the front lines and offered her body for stress relief to the scared and weary.

Phoebe stretched forth her long legs and laid down next to Sipho to catch a few hours of sleep before the battle started all over again.

Ndlovu and Izzie huddled together with Alpheus and Sarah as they tried to find a solution. Eerie cries were heard on the veldt and they could only hope it was their allies doing their best to divide and conquer. The baboons successfully removed the food supplies from the wagons and were busy transporting them to the fortress.

They chattered and laughed as they helped themselves to copious amounts of food and alcoholic drink. Ndlovu wondered if there would be any food left for the defenders at the end of the night.

Ammunition was uplifted by monkeys and bush babies. Crocodiles stopped the soldiers from refilling their water supplies and hippos trampled any fire lit near the distant water holes and rivers. They had decided even though they would not join the fight, it did not hurt them to do their bit if the enemy encroached on their own domain.

By morning no one had slept much, but there was at least a glimmer of hope as they observed the soldiers. Small groups were separated from the main ranks and were now open to the ministrations of the wild dogs. The main groups were significantly reduced and limited in their ability to be a threat. Some soldiers retreated and commanders were forced to use violence to turn them around.

The defenders on the other hand, had no significant damage. Apart from being sleep deprived and tired, they had all eaten a good breakfast and were ready for the battle ahead. The baboons had left a few choice scraps of food the families could use. The baboons on the other hand nursed hang overs from the alcohol and were extremely grumpy with all and sundry. They retreated to their rocky cliffs with a promise of further assistance as long as the noise was not too loud and did not impact on their aching heads and disturbed stomachs.

Ndlovu and Alpheus surveyed their families and the troops.

"We can beat them you know, Alpheus. We are still strong enough to do this. Logistically we have them cornered without food or ammunition for their larger guns. We have come across this bunch before. They came into our kingdom and shot a family of baboons just for the fun of seeing animals bleed to death. I promised my family that they would never be allowed back to terrorise us again."

Alpheus had wondered why the elephant people had been so eager to help them and this explained a lot.

Nodding his head in agreement he said, "Yup, but what if they come back when we're not as strong as we are now? Maybe we should ask the women what they think?"

The elephant soldiers were eager to see the enemy defeated and suggested that the Zulu army be given a sound whipping and sent on their way. "We can do it boss, without breaking a sweat."

The women had stayed silent during this discussion. Then Nyoni stepped forward and raised her voice. "Soldiers, family, friends and animals far and wide. What can we do to guarantee that these thugs do not come back and hurt our little ones when we are unprepared? If we can make them feel that they have won a small victory, they might be happy to leave. Violence solves the problem today, but what about tomorrow? Can we not try to broker a peace treaty that will suit us all?"

A few people shook their heads in disagreement, but then Izzie stepped forward and stood next to Nyoni. "We were lucky to escape without injury or death, and yes, we could beat them and send them packing, but they have a huge army at their beck and call. I vote with Nyoni. Negotiations all the way."

Thandi linked arms with Nyoni and Izzie and a few of the other women joined them. "Let's take a vote. After all it is our lives that are on the line and the lives of our children and friends." she declared.

A few people grumbled at this strange way of waging a war, but finally all agreed to at least give it a try. Some hoped that the Zulu would not be open to a peace deal and felt that they would get to fight anyway, while others put their faith in the women. The vote was a simple aye or nay. With those for the peace deal outnumbering the fighters by only two votes. A close call, but one they could all live with.

CHAPTER SIX

Nyoni went to the General of the enemy army to broker the peace agreement. She flew in as an eagle and changed into a woman in front of the men, who were shocked at her arrival. She was decked out by the elephants in a beautiful suit of armour made from copper, shining in the sun. In her one hand was a short stabbing spear and in the other a white flag of peace.

"General I'm here for your own good and to see how we can resolve this impasse amicably." She spoke softly but firmly.

Crossing her legs, she sank to the ground elegantly. The General signalled to a soldier to bring forth a chair for him. Taking his antelope tail whisk in his hand, he pointed it at Nyoni. "Why should I broker a peace agreement? We're winning and you're running scared, otherwise you wouldn't want to speak peace or are you wanting to surrender?"

Nyoni smiled. "Let me show you the bigger picture, General." She changed into a Lammergeyer and grabbed the shocked General by his shoulders, Nyoni flew high above the plains until the distant horizon curved across the sky.

"There to the left is what is left of your elite Royal troops. Less than twenty able to fight. And to the right we have your war contraptions. Please note there is no ammunition to fire on us. These men are hungry and tired. The only strength you had was your air ships and they're now reduced to barely three. I say barely because of those three, two need major repairs. Do you still think you're winning, General?"

Nyoni dropped him back on the ground gently and then transformed into her human form. "Let's talk, General.

Here are the conditions we feel are essential. One, you and your men leave this valley as soon as possible, perhaps within the next hour or so. Two, we make an agreement that no harm will come to the people in this area by your hand or the hands of your minions. Three, we'll return any injured men to you, so you may take them with you and finally, free safe passage for the Air Whisperers out of the area."

Nyoni pulled a large piece of papyrus paper from her armour and a pen from a pouch on her back and offered them to the General to sign. She did not have high hopes all the promises would be kept, but it was worth a try.

"I demand to speak to your General. I'll not make agreements with women of low rank. Your demands are unreasonable anyway. The ammunition can be found, men can be fed and my soldiers will be pleased to fight on until we've obtained our objective." He lifted his chin up in a defiant gesture and then turned his back on Nyoni.

Ndlovu and Izzie rose from the grass next to Nyoni while Alpheus, and Thandi materialised beside her.

"General. We're here." Ndlovu's deep rumble of a voice vibrated from the toes to the crown of each of their heads and Nyoni smiled to see the shock on the General's face as he spun around.

"Where did you freaks come from? Sonne g'Nyoga you've no respect for the might and power of the Royal guard." He scowled and frowned at the group and his fingers twitched towards his Kalashnikov rifle leaning against a nearby Fever tree. He paced around the chair he had leaned against.

With a glare at the people before him, he sat down with as much finesse as he could manage in the circumstances. Too late he realised if he sat down he would be lower than the others. Making the best of a bad situation he pointed his switch at Ndlovu. "Speak. Only you, none of these other misfits."

Ndlovu rumbled a laugh and pointed at Nyoni. "Didn't my compatriot show you the foolishness of your aggression? I'm sure she could be persuaded to take you higher, so you can appreciate the majesty of the land you're desecrating."

With a snap of his fingers, over one hundred men rose from the grasslands, each of them holding a captive in front of them. The captives were bound with rawhide ropes and blindfolded with cloths and ready for surrender as long as they could be allowed to leave.

"Behold your soldiers, General."

With another snap of his fingers the men vanished into the earth. It was an amazing trick the Elephant people had perfected over many millennia. They did not actually vanish, but rather dropped down into a system of underground tunnels. Each entry hole was covered with a trap door and it was the General's bad luck he had camped close to one of these tunnel entrances.

As the captives dropped into the holes they let out a scream of pure terror, adding to the sense of drama. The screams came from the very bowels of the earth they had been standing on.

The General was shaken, but still did not want to admit defeat without winning some sort of victory he could take to his king. "I demand hostages to take with me. I'll release them once we've left this valley safely, but only if all my men are returned unhurt."

Ndlovu and Alpheus looked at each other and shook their heads in unison. "UNACCEPTABLE." They both roared in tandem.

The impasse meant they might have to continue the fight and they might not be as lucky to escape serious injury as they had been the day before.

"I'll go as a hostage." Sipho stepped out of one of the trap doors. "I can't control the air, so they'll have no use for me once we've left the valley. I don't want anyone else to be hurt."

Thandi put her hand over her mouth as she tried to suppress a cry of anguish. Another child stepped forward from a trap door. "Send me. I can go."

This time it was Izzie who had to stop herself crying out as her daughter Tembe stepped lightly to the front. Taking Sipho by the hand, the two teenagers stood proudly, offering themselves as a sacrifice for their families. The parents looked at each other and then at their children.

They went over in their minds all the pros and cons of this agreement. They did not trust the Zulu General, but knew it was a way of avoiding more conflict and they were already making plans in their heads to retrieve the children as soon as possible.

The General put his hand forward to take the agreement and the pen from Nyoni. Not a word was uttered as he signed his name and then all the other parties put their names to the document. He snapped his fingers and his henchmen took a child each by the arm and marched them to the rear of the camp. Izzie and Thandi both clamped their teeth down on cries of anguish.

Ndlovu and Alpheus looked at their children with pride as the two youngsters did not flinch or cry out as they were roughly restrained and placed in a wagon.

By lunch time the soldiers marched through the mountain passes. Nyoni, Thandi, Phoebe and Sarah watched as they flew through the air and Izzie stood sentinel on the ramparts of her fortress with tears streaming down her face and her mouth in a tight line.

Alpheus and Ndlovu huddled together over their purloined map working on strategies to distract themselves from the fate of their children. Already making plans to steal them back if the Zulu did not keep their promise. They could use attrition by sending troops to attack their convoy, but this would endanger the children. They could lead them into blind canyons by blocking the way, thus making them easy targets for attack, but again it was the children who would pay the ultimate price.

It all depended on how well the children were being guarded and if there was a possibility of spiriting them away unseen. The Zulu were famous for their pincer battle tactics known as the horns of the bull. The main concentration of troops was held in the centre while two horns of soldiers were sent out to encircle the enemy. They would need to either use this to their own advantage or else put them in a position where they were unable to deploy this manoeuvre.

Thandi, Nyoni and Sarah reported back before dusk informing the others that the army had set up camp outside the boundaries of the kingdom of the Elephants and had shown no sign of releasing the children.

They were kept in a hastily constructed boma of thorn bushes in the very centre of the troops. They had been fed, but not given anything to sleep on. They both looked healthy and showed no signs of discomfit.

The children huddled together finding warmth in each other. Thandi changed herself into a scattering of petals and drifted down into their boma, but it had been too dangerous to materialise, as soldiers stood guard. Sipho had known his mother was there with them and had whispered they were fine and would wait for their parents to come and get them.

Izzie was relieved to hear this as she knew her headstrong daughter was more than capable of trying to escape.

CHAPTER SEVEN

In the thorn bush boma Tembe woke from a deep sleep and sat bolt upright. Her heart beat madly in her chest and she lifted her nose to the air. Smoke. Lots of smoke. She shook Sipho awake. "Trouble. I think the soldiers have set fire to something big."

They stood, looking at the horizon towards the Elephant kingdom and saw a glow smudge the sky. The soldiers were all looking the same way and Sipho whispered, "I think it's time for us to go."

Grabbing Tembe's hand they dug a shallow ditch below the boma using the plates from their meagre meal. Barely deep enough for them both to wriggle through. They were worried they might be seen and stopped, but the Zulu soldiers were too focused on the glow over the horizon. Sipho made it out first and Tembe was not far behind him, they crouched down low and then made their way as fast as they could to the deep jungle to the South. Sipho might not be able to walk on air, but he had compensated for his lack of talent in the area of flying, by becoming a climber of trees.

Pulling Tembe up a forest giant, they were soon able to look into the distance as well as observe their captors. Their escape had not been noticed and the soldiers were in a celebratory mood. The soldiers danced around the fire singing and making feints with their assegais. Their songs were all about the great victory they had over the Elephant people and how brave they had been. Two soldiers were lifted up on shoulders as being the fire bearers of the Zulu.

The General sat on a large chair surveying the troops and drinking copious amounts of beer from a large calabash. He wobbled to his feet and started shouting above the revelry.

"Tonight, we've defeated those who thought they were cleverer than us. They thought they could shame us into leaving, but we're the ones who are laughing now. Their home is ash and is in ruins. We can only hope none were left alive." A great cheer went up and Sipho and Tembe held each other tight.

"You're my only family now, Sipho, and I'm yours. Together we'll avenge the innocent victims and punish the guilty." Her eyes shone with tears, her chin high.

It was time for them to leave and put some distance between themselves and the soldiers. Their options were to find the grandparents and aunts and uncles from either of their families. Sipho knew his family were too close to the seat of power, Ulundi and it would not be safe.

Neither of them wanted to say they were concerned what their future might hold. Tembe had to swallow the lump in her throat a few times before she could speak. "We could always travel to my Uncle. He lives in Mozambique." She winced, "But it's so far away and I'm not exactly sure where he is." They looked deep into each other's eyes and announced together. "Mozambique."

But first they needed to see if there were any survivors of the dreadful fire. Tembe knew a pass not on any maps and safe from detection by the soldiers. Staying in the protection of the jungle trees they worked their way towards their destination.

Tembe used her superior hearing to listen for danger. Twice they needed to climb a tree to avoid people. Both times it had been a stranger and not the soldiers in pursuit and they were able to avoid detection.

As the sun rose through the clouds of smoke, they reached the top of the mountain and could look down at the devastation. Birds of prey flew in lazy circles in the chill morning air, circling carcasses of dead antelope and other animals killed by the conflagration.

The children found a small hollow in the rocks fed by a sweet spring and drank their fill of the refreshing water. Sipho and Tembe sat for about an hour to see if they could see any movement, but it was the vultures and hyenas on the move.

The rock walls of the fortress were still standing, but badly burned in places. The scars of the battles and the fire bled across the plains as great thorn trees lay in ashes and the grasslands were black stubble where once had been lush grass and bushes.

Sipho asked quietly, "Do we really want to go down there, Tembe? I think my heart will break if I have to see any of my family burnt or killed."

Tembe grabbed his shoulder. "Of course, we want to go down there, what if someone needs our help? What if they're hiding somewhere underground or even in the lake and hoping someone will come and find them. If they're dead we've a duty to bury them." Her eyes filled with tears, but she was determined to do her duty.

They waited for night fall in case any of the soldiers were still in the vicinity. They saw a few soldiers on the periphery about lunchtime, but the soldiers soon left.

As the shadows grew longer, the two children descended from the mountain top into the fields of burnt stubble. Their feet created little puffs of black soot as they walked in silence, too scared to say what they feared they might find.

Lions feasted on the dead animals and they were careful to avoid them. The lions were so sated they barely looked at the two scrawny humans, but they felt they should be safe and kept their distance anyway.

A hyena came and sniffed them. They stumbled into a cheetah who had dragged a dead antelope into a partially burnt tree. But neither were interested in them as a meal and they continued in stunned silence. The grass was harsh on their feet and they were soon covered in ash from head to toe.

The fortress loomed in front of them at last and Tembe walked into the courtyard and called, "Mom, Dad, anyone, are you there?"

Sipho walked around calling for his family. Finally, they heard a groan and followed the sound and found Alpheus lying crumpled next to the lake. Both his legs had been snapped and he was covered in bruises but he was alive at least.

Tembe took a cloth torn from her skirt and dipped it in the water and gently cleaned the soot from his face.

"It was awful. We were all asleep when the smoke got to us. Thandi, Nyoni, Sarah and Phoebe tried to spirit the children away to somewhere safe, but they never came back and I don't know if they found somewhere before the flames came."

He looked at Tembe and informed her, "Your parents managed to get some of the children underground and then they went out to try and battle the flames by clearing the grass and brush from the edges of the fortress. They're still busy putting out small fires. I'm injured because the wildebeest stampeded and ran right through the centre of the courtyard. Unfortunately, I was in their way. I managed to pull myself to the edge of the lake so at least I could have water, but it's been a long, long day for us all." He tried to laugh, but stopped when he realised it caused his ribs to ache.

Sipho wondered why his mother and the others had not returned to look for his father. Tembe and Sipho worked to make Alpheus more comfortable. Tembe raced to the underground tunnels and found some of the children there, too scared to come out.

They had food and drink and many of the little ones curled up and slept on the bare ground. Tembe collected a blanket and some food and took it back to Alpheus. She carefully helped him onto the blanket and then Sipho and Tembe each took a corner and slowly dragged him towards the safety of the tunnels.

To get him down the stairs would have been too painful, so they gave him the food to eat and then laid down next to him to stand guard for the remainder of the night.

As the sky lightened, Ndlovu and Izzie returned. Their eyes bloodshot and their hands hung at their sides in defeat. Izzie cried when she saw Tembe safe and rushed forward to take her in her arms.

Ndlovu immediately noticed Alpheus and rushed over to help. "Willow bark. Do we have any willow bark, Izzie?"

Izzie and Tembe searched for supplies safe and had escaped the fire and soon came back with a bag of medicines to help. Ndlovu looked around to see where the Air Whisperer women were and was surprised not to find them close by.

He knew Nyoni had the power to ease pain with a touch and wondered what could keep her away from her husband at a time like this.

He took Sipho aside. "Do you know where they are?" The boy shrugged his shoulder and shook his head.

"No sir, they went to take the children to safety and haven't returned. I'm worried about them in case they flew into a trap and are unable to come back."

A deep rumble like a drum was emitted from the chest of Ndlovu and he raised his great ears to the skies as he waited for a reply.

He tried all four corners of the compass and soon a sound so soft and gentle it was difficult to hear with normal ears, quivered through the air. But Ndlovu had no problem hearing and turned to Alpheus to tell him the news.

"They were captured. All of them, but they're unharmed. It wasn't the soldiers who caught them, but rather the wood sprites near the great Ubombo. You, my dear friend, are too injured to travel far, but I'll send my best young men to find and save your family while you stay here and recover."

Alpheus tried to raise himself up, but was forced to admit defeat as he sunk down once more. "I want Sipho to go with them. They know him and he can talk to them in the special air language."

Even the short speech tired Alpheus and he closed his eyes for a moment. "Promise me you'll do your best, but if it gets too dangerous, come find me and we'll try together again when I'm better. Promise with all your heart you'll do this for me."

"I'll be your eyes and your ears, your arms and your hands, strong in defence of our family. But I'll use my mind to find the best way to achieve this as if you were standing next to me advising me."

The twelve-year-old boy shed his childish ways in such a short time Alpheus felt sad for the loss of innocence. He patted Sipho's hand and nodded his head.

CHAPTER EIGHT

They made Sipho a coat of armour from the finest metals available to the Elephant people. The family sat together weaving together chain mail, while others hammered at the anvil to make it as thin as possible so Sipho would have ease of movement.

Tembe collected a thick leopard skin blanket from her rooms and wrapped all his supplies in it. A knife was attached to the thigh of the chain mail and a crossbow such as had never before been seen by the Air Whisperers. The quill pen could be used to shoot a poisonous dart, the belt became a garrotte and even a parchment could be set alight and burn so hot it would melt metal.

Tembe stood beside Sipho as he prepared to leave. Three young men metamorphosed into elephants so Sipho could ride on their backs. As he jumped nimbly onto the back of the leading elephant, he did not see Tembe change into her own pachyderm shape.

She was smaller than the others, but kept pace with ease. They walked in the general area the message had come from and only stopped when it was too dark to see their way. As Sipho slipped from the back of the elephant he saw Tembe standing there and was astonished she would risk her life for his family.

"Why did you come, Tembe? Surely you would want to stay with your family to help them?"

"Didn't I tell you, you were my family? Family stand together and I'm standing with you."

She produced a calabash of nuts and berries and handed around a few handfuls to each of the men. Then as they sat around in the dark, each person introduced themselves.

"My name is Xele. I'm here because I've fought in battles before and can help train you." He was black as the night and as thin as a rake with shining grey eyes.

"My name is Isifunda. I'm a master of stealth and can enter places without others knowing." Isifunda wore thick glasses and peered at everything with a great intensity. He was shorter than the other two but his muscles were by far the most impressive of the trio.

"I'm Bala. You don't need to know what I do, I'll make sure you're kept safe." Bala had a large scar across his cheek and across his eye and into his hairline. A dimple peeped out each time he grinned and he grinned all the time.

Tembe stood. "I'm a princess in my tribe. In our tribe it's the women who are leaders. So, I'm here to see if I can, one day, take the lead from my mother. And also, because we don't believe in allowing innocent people to be taken in traps by our neighbours. Now we must sleep, we leave at first light."

Sipho was amazed. He had never heard of a woman being in charge. How very strange, he thought as his head found a soft spot in the leopard skin blanket. The next thing he knew he was being shaken awake by Tembe.

"Come on, sleepy head. The sun is already rising and we've work to do this day."

No breakfast was offered, but Tembe must have realised Sipho could not survive on leaves and grasses like the elephants could and threw him the calabash with the nuts and berries. The little group were soon at the edge of an eerie forest shifting and moving in amongst the trees to avoid leaving an obvious path.

The branches dipped towards the ground and roots pushed up through the earth. At closer inspection some of the trees were men in camouflage. They were painted and coloured to match exactly the leaves around them and the deception was enhanced by their clothing covered with living plants.

Tembe walked to the largest tree blocking their path. "Oh, great and wonderful sprites of the forest, I'm here for your help. I'm Tembe, daughter of the beautiful and wise Izzie, queen of all the elephants, kind and generous to those she considers her friends, but answers threat with an iron fist. Some of our friends have landed on your trees as they fled the great fire and we're here to offer them passage back to our land."

The forest dwellers advanced aggressively on Tembe and Sipho could feel his companions prepare for battle. No weapon was exposed, but the armaments were close to hand. Leaves waved backwards and forwards and a flurry of leaves formed into an old man, so wizened he looked like he would blow over in a strong breeze.

Tembe stayed where she was and waited for the old man to come closer.

"They landed in my trees without permission. They need to pay a price. We'll give them back when they've done penance, such is the law of this land."

"Are you telling me you don't welcome travellers to your realm?" Asked Tembe. "Not even fugitives from the crazy king of the Zulus? The same king would chop down your trees with no thought to you and your lives. These are women and children who don't mean you harm. What type of penance do you expect them to do?" She glared at the old man and crossed her arms across her chest.

"Come, we'll discuss this more at our camp."

The trees separated and revealed a clear roadway through the forest. It did not sound like a good idea to Sipho to put all their trust in this ancient dried out husk of a man. Bala was nowhere to be seen. If the old man noticed the departure of the third elephant, he didn't say a word and led the way with a measured step.

On either side of the road the trees kept pace with them. Many of them were covered in vicious barbs and would no doubt be extremely effective in a battle. The trees gradually became rounded and softer. Colourful bark on their trunks. These must be the women, or did trees have gender? He was not quite sure and tried not to look directly at any tree for too long in case he caused offence.

Xele and Isifunda flanked the two children as they came to a large clearing surrounded by tall stands of bamboo. The old man introduced himself as E'Showe and offered them a green tea to drink. Sipho wanted to decline, but saw each of the others in his party taking small sips from the bowls they had been offered. It tasted of moss and lichen mixed with a rich flavoured honey. The flavour was not unpleasant and Sipho took another sip before putting his bowl down on the ground next to him.

He looked around but couldn't see any sign of his family until a few rose petals swirling around his feet. "Hi, Mom." he whispered.

One of the petals brushed his hand and then sank down with the others as Thandi listened to the negotiations in her petal form.

E'Showe clicked his fingers and they were surrounded by one hundred men, all dressed in shades of green and holding fighting sticks in their hands. Alpheus would have loved one of those sticks but it was no time to admire the weapons of their hosts.

"Our friends, we'd like to see they are unharmed. E'Showe, could you have someone bring them here?" Thembe stated.

"Don't dare to be so impudent, child. This is my domain and you'll wait for the time we decree. First we'll decide on a punishment and then we'll talk about what happens next." Declared E'Showe.

Tembe signalled for a chair which was brought forth by two men. They placed the chair, made from vines twisted and curled in a curious way, behind her. Tembe sat, arranging her clothes around her and made sure her small spear was easily accessible. She crossed her legs delicately and leaned her wrists on her knees.

"Our families have lived together in harmony for many generations, E'Showe. Can't we come to an amicable agreement? We'll happily do your bidding in payment for your mercy. I'm authorised to use my men to clear weeds from the forest floor, or drag logs to clear dead trees from paths."

It took another two hours of negotiations to resolve the problem to the benefit of them all. The Elephant people brought a dozen steel bowls to the forest as well as the other work promised. The forest sprites would agree to release the Air Whisperers if they would sign a document to say they would never return.

"E'Showe, I'm sure the Air Whisperers will have no problem with these conditions. It's not like they travelled here on purpose. We're prepared to repair whatever damage you consider important to you and your family." Tembe assured.

"Yes, there are many things we have suffered from this invasion. Women were forced to run and hide. The men were busy with important work and this work suffered because of the Air Whisperers. Terrible when our home is under threat. Awful. This is stuff to be fixed with a few moments work or a few trinkets? This will affect our peace for many years to come."

Tembe almost rolled her eyes at this blatant dramatic over statement.

"E'Showe, we apologise for this imposition. But this will go a small way to heal the hurt. And in the future, we'll work alongside you to continue to fix what has been damaged. You know we're people who keep our promises." Tembe smiled at the old man and hoped he would accept the terms of the contract.

Heads shook in agreement and the wood sprites were agreeable with the discussion. In fact, many of them appeared to be more than pleased and had grins spreading over their faces in a suspicious manner.

The night was not far off and E'Showe announced, "It'll be difficult to get the Air Whisperers to the camp before dark. Maybe you should think about staying the night." He suggested to Tembe.

Xele leaned down and whispered something quietly to Tembe. She patted Xele on his shoulder and Sipho wondered what it was all about.

Wooden bowls of fruit were brought to a grass mat in the middle of the camp. Steaming pots of madumbes were brought in by some of the men. A large container of spicy beans and bowls of vegetables were placed before them. Tembe held her group back with a tiny gesture of her wrist.

"Our hosts have done us proud with all this delicious food. We insist you, E'Showe, enjoy it first." Tembe declared with a no-nonsense manner. She was not about to allow her men to be poisoned. They might have negotiated a peace treaty, but the trust was still not there. E'Showe laughed and spooned out a huge helping of food onto his wooden plate. Looking directly at Tembe, he ceremoniously ate a spoonful.

Feeling a little ashamed, the elephant people and Sipho joined the others at the meal. They had not eaten all day and were more than ready to do the food justice. As Sipho was about to ladle the first mouthful, he saw the rose petals rise up and settle on his shoulder.

A voice so soft it might be mistaken for the sound of the breeze as it sighed, "The food isn't poisoned, but your spoons have been coated with a sleeping draught. I overheard them talking earlier and they plan to hand us over to the Zulu king for the reward. Beware son, be careful."

Sipho leaned close to Tembe and passed on this message. He stood behind the other two men. "Pretend to eat. Fake the symptoms of a sleeping draught. Don't give away the game guys." They all managed to avoid using the spoons.

Xele and Isifunda ate with their hands and Tembe and Sipho followed their examples. Pretending to eat a small amount with the spoons, letting their heads drop down onto their chests. Xele even managed a few grunts and snores for good effect.

Tembe slipped from her chair onto the ground as elegantly as she could. Sipho was the last to pretend he was sleepy, but first he wobbled his way to the edge of the clearing and the forest sprites laughed as he tried to relieve himself before falling into the bushes. As he fell he saw Bala standing behind a tree as still as a shadow.

The forest sprites ate and drank for what felt like hours before they too succumbed to sleep. Bala waited a short while before he stepped quietly from his hiding place. Sipho tested his fingers as the pins and needles of being immobile slowly dissipated. Xele, Isifunda and Sipho quickly tied up their enemies and as they did this, Thandi appeared in her human form.

"The women and children aren't far away, but we need stealth because the guards are still awake and armed."

Xele smiled a wicked smile. "Good, I feel like a good fight."

Bala and Thandi led the way down a path they had not noticed before. "Let's hope there aren't more forest sprites hiding away." Tembe said quietly.

The women and children of the Air Whisperers were in a cage with bars so closely woven there was no way for even the smallest hummingbird to find its way through. Two large men in forest marched up and down on opposite sides of the cage.

Bala signalled to Xele and Isifunda to take the closest guard down, once he had crept around the trees and was in position on the other side of the clearing. Stepping up silently behind the guard he snapped his neck in one fluid motion.

The other guard sensed some movement because he raised a whistle to his lips when the blade Xele held found its way into his back. Isifunda clasped his hand over the man's mouth to stop him calling out. The whole manoeuvre took barely a minute.

Tembe, Sipho and Thandi were busy loosening the bindings on the cage door, when a shrill sound rang through the forest.

The alarm was given. Someone heard their movements, no matter how quiet they had thought they were being. The three large elephant men surrounded Sipho as he struggled to free his family. Tembe handed him her stabbing spear and within seconds he had the cords cut.

Thandi took the hands of two of the children and in the twinkling of an eye she spirited them away. Nyoni and Sarah took children in their hands and even Phoebe danced through the air. She offered to help Tembe and Sipho to escape, but neither one of them were prepared to leave their compatriots behind to face the wrath of the forest sprites.

The forest was alive with the rustle of leaves. The pathways blocked and they were cornered with no visible chance of escape. The elephant men were not to be outdone and changed into their pachyderm personas. They charged the forest walls. They uprooted the trees in their way and threw them at any advancing soldiers.

Ghastly screams shook the air, but the elephants continued with their rampage. Sipho jumped to the back of Xele and lashed wildly with his weapons to stop any sprite from attacking from above. He was glad to see a few sprites clutching injured arms and legs but did not stop to admire his handiwork.

All the anger from the past few days came out like a roaring wind and he issued a war cry from the bottom of his being. Anger for all those animals left dead by the Zulu soldiers when they burnt the land, anger at having to flee from his home in terror of their lives, and anger his friends had to be subjected to all this animosity through no fault of their own.

His eyes clouded with a blood red mist and he slashed indiscriminately at anything moving. He kept the image of his injured father in front of him to keep the fatigue from slowing him down. Slash, cut, chop and scream, and the forest opened in front of him. Sipho did not feel the hits from the fighting sticks, the pricks of thorns or barbs, there was nothing stopping him now.

For a moment they feared they would have to continue the battle through the whole night, but soon they could see the safety of the grasslands and in front of the forest, arrayed in glistening armour, one hundred elephants stood sentinel. Even the smallest elephant was decked out in shining armour and holding small spears in readiness.

Sipho had been injured at some stage because he could feel liquid dripping down his arms. Unable to see much in the cover of the forest, he continued fighting, but now he could take a breath and assess the damage. The adrenaline pumped through his body and he felt the shivering in his arms and legs as his body tried to process it all.

Stepping into the moonlight, Sipho glanced down at his body to inspect the wounds. But there were none. Miraculously the liquid dripping off him was caused not by injuries, but rather by sweat flowing like a river. Sipho laughed hysterically.

Xele reached up with his trunk and deposited Sipho on the ground.

"Mate, if you're going to wet yourself laughing, you had better do it somewhere else rather than on my back."

This made Sipho laugh even more as he gripped his sides and doubled over with mirth.

PART TWO
REBUILDING

CHAPTER NINE

There was no way Alpheus and his family could return to their own village. Ndlovu suggested they stay for a while until Alpheus's broken legs were stronger. The tribes worked together to build a series of huts outside the walls of the fortress.

Much of the local wood was burnt or charred and it required many trips to the mountains to find suitable wood. The grasses of the veldt recovered quickly and soon was tall enough to be harvested to form coverings for the huts.

Sipho and two of his younger brothers took responsibility for finding a safe place for their cattle to graze. Phoebe taught two of her sisters how to milk the cows and each morning balanced clay pots on their heads as they walked to and from the cattle. Their mothers handed over the workload to their children as they themselves created clothes from what they could grow. A small crop of cotton, a cave full of mushrooms made into a leather substitute and grasses woven to form intricate skirts.

The boys returned to their ancestral habit of wearing a beshu made from some of the skins of the dead animals killed by the fire. Classes were held for reading and writing. Sarah stepped into the role of teacher for the younger group. Alpheus set up a class for maths and science with some afterhours training for those who wanted to try their hand at stick fighting.

Ndlovu opened his workshops to all those who wanted to learn the art of working with steel. The forge filled with eager people asking a thousand and one questions. Phoebe took to the work and was often found late at night bent over a piece of steel. She twisted and turned the metal into mechanical shapes with internal workings leaving Ndlovu in awe of her vision. Her Air Whispering skills included controlling the air and she used this to great effect as she manipulated the forge to her needs.

By the end of six months Alpheus's legs were as good as they would ever be. He needed to walk using a stick when ascending hills, but on the level, he could move with speed and dexterity. His three wives rubbed ointments on his scars and they healed. One result of his injury was he could now predict the approaching storms and how severe they would be. His left big toe was the predictor of floods and a general ache in both legs meant a gentle rain would last for days.

Ndlovu and Izzie never showed any need for the family to move on and were content to co-exist with the Air Whisperers. The Zulu warriors could sometimes be seen at the top of mountain passes looking at their industry through spy glasses. So far none of them had ventured onto the plains and the families became complacent and security was relaxed.

It was a complete surprise when one morning Sipho came in from where the cattle were kept and complained about Phoebe and the girls not milking the cows. The family searched the forge and the surrounding fields but no sign was found of the girls.

Nyoni flew into the sky like an eagle and scoured the countryside in search of her eldest child. Her enhanced vision picked up a track through the grasslands. Indistinct but clear to those who knew what to look for. The bent over grasses, the broken twigs. From what Nyoni could ascertain, the girls were not putting up any sort of fight and this worried her more than anything. By the time the alarm was raised the girls were gone for hours and the abductors had made good their escape.

Ndlovu sent out a message and he listened to the response from animals on the plains.

"They were given knock out drops as far as my people can tell. They say the girls are asleep but smell strange and think it's the residue of a spray of some sort. They were taken at first light and it appears to be Zulu warriors who are responsible."

Alpheus sat with his wives and they planned a strategy of attack and recovery. The girls were now inside a mechanical form of transport easy to follow, but surrounded by many soldiers armed to the teeth. Nyoni was able to see though the bars of the clanking truck and spied the girls crumpled on the floor. Attack would be foolish and recovery almost impossible without endangering them with no guarantee of success. Alpheus felt they should sneak up and tie up whom they could and steal their guns.

"We're tired of fighting, dear husband. Isn't there another way?"

"Nyoni, we all know Phoebe will look after the little ones and if she gets a moment to escape safely then she will. Thandi, can you follow them? Talk to them when you can."

Alpheus knew his two older wives would be more able to cope with the stress as they could do something to help.

"Please, please bring them back safely. I can't imagine life without my little girl." Sarah wailed with tears streaming down her cheeks.

"Come sweetheart, you're stronger than you know and we'll move heaven and earth to bring our girls home." Alpheus put his arm around Sarah in an attempt to comfort her, but she cried until she was gasped with sobs and shook from head to toe.

"No, Alpheus, you can't understand. She came from my body and I've been with her every moment of her life. I wish I'd never let her go off with the others to milk the cows. It's all my fault. I should have been a better mother. I should have gone with them. I know I should've done more. I'm useless. I can't even offer to save them by fighting the soldiers. I don't deserve to be a mother. Aaargh." Sarah collapsed on the floor in a heap sobbing her heart out in self-castigation and worry.

Alpheus knew any words now would only make things worse.

Nyoni and Thandi had tears in their own eyes, but blaming others or themselves would not help the girls in their predicament.

Nyoni gave Alpheus and Thandi a hug and took to the air, flying high above the land to follow her daughter. She knew it helped if she was doing something constructive, sitting crying was not an option.

Thandi gave Alpheus a hug and whispered. "Sarah will be fine in a while. Let her cry for a bit longer and then ask her to look after the other children. Give her a job where she can keep her mind off the kidnapping. Stay strong, husband, and we will do what we can. Soon we'll be back with a report and once we know where we stand we can better plan what to do." She changed into dust particles and a breeze lifted her into the air towards Ulundi and her daughter.

"I'm coming Phoebe, Rachel and Maria but you need to be strong. No time for hysterics." She tried to assure herself as she whispered positive comments.

"They'll be happy and safe and I'll be able to whisk them away in the blink of an eye. I can see them through the bars of the wagon and they smell awful, but still alive and breathing. Breathing is good. Drugged is not. Oh, pull yourself together woman, now is not the time to lose your cool."

Both women kept pace with the soldiers. They held back and waited to see if there was any possibility of escape.

Thandi slipped through the bars of the vehicle and settled on the bench next to Phoebe. She would be there when the girls woke up. The day stretched endlessly for the family left behind. Nyoni flew back at dusk and kept them updated on what was happening. She ate a small meal and then flew out as an owl through the darkening sky.

CHAPTER TEN

The vehicle travelled through the night. As dawn rose they reached Ulundi and the Zulu royal courts. Phoebe, Rachel and little Maria woke disorientated as the soldiers shook them roughly. Phoebe woke first and it took a moment to figure out where they were. She reached out and brushed her fingers over her sisters' skin. They looked around with big eyes at the soldiers who leered at them.

One moment they had been in the fields laughing and joking about cows and the dew on the grasses. Now they were being gripped by large dark visaged men with evil in their eyes.

Maria reached for her big sister and shook with fear as she took in the strange world around her. She could only catch glimpses of the countryside outside the bars of the vehicle and it was definitely not the grasslands or even her beloved forests. This was more like a city with buildings and loud noises of a mechanical nature and even the air smelled strange.

"Where's Mom and Dad? I'm scared, Phoebe. Can we go home now, please?"

Tears ran down Maria's face and dripped off her chin. Rachel and Phoebe looked at each other with eyes so full of trepidation and terror at what their fate would be.

Phoebe pulled back her shoulders. She was now the adult and it was her job to keep her sisters safe. No parents to turn to, nobody to blame if things didn't work out, now was a time to step up and be like Auntie Mary. No Scaredy Phoebe, think what their parents would have them do in this situation and go ahead and do it to the best of her ability. She hoped it would be enough.

They were taken to rooms and instructed to clean themselves up and eat something as they were to be presented to the Mother of the King.

Flower petals floated through the air with them as they stumbled along the passageways. Never had they seen such decadence. Chairs covered with silk cushions, tables made from exotic hardwoods, floors of semi-precious stones and walls covered with embossed papers. The palace was stunning and if they had not been prisoners they might have enjoyed the skill and crafts employed. As it was, they had eyes only for the gold toilet and shower with crystal knobs.

They took turns cleaning themselves up and ridding themselves of the stench of the drugs they had been sprayed with. On the bed were dresses made of delicate fine material so fine it was difficult to see where the seams had been sewn. Gossamer fine and gorgeously decorated dresses fitting them all perfectly.

Two guards stayed in the room with the girls and were tactful enough to turn their backs as Phoebe dressed herself. Thandi entered the shower with each girl and whispered words of support and encouragement before vanishing in a puff of air and returned to her fellow wives to report back.

The three girls were taken to the audience room where Atalia reclined on a low couch covered in embroidered silks in a rainbow of colours. She waved her hand in the air to beckon them forward and assessed them with a brief look.

"Good day, my cousins. I'm so glad you accepted the invitation to visit the Royal courts." As Phoebe opened her mouth to say something angry in response, Atalia held her hand out and continued on. "Maybe not the best way for an invitation to be given, I agree, but your family weren't responding to other incentives to visit me."

A servant brought forward three seats for the youngsters to sit on and proceeded to place a large tray of fruit and nuts in front of them.

"Eat, eat. You must be famished after your ordeal yesterday." Flicking her long-painted nails towards the servants, they immediately jumped to attention and brought forth further treats. Men with oiled bodies like copper and women, with very little clothing on, swarmed around the room; adjusting tables, curtains, fans and attending to anything the Queen ordered.

"Tell me how your dear father is? I heard he was trampled by animals and broke his legs. I hope he received competent treatment. Your family are to blame and if I'm forced to use unsavoury methods it's because they're so stubborn. What shall I do with you three? I'm tempted to give you to my soldiers to use for their amusement."

Atalia peered at Maria and pulled a disgusted face. She ran a scarlet nail down the young girl's cheek and then pinched her mercilessly until she raised a red welt on Maria's face. Maria bit the inside of her lip to stop the scream.

"No, not today, but maybe later. I do have some men who love the younger girls for their sport and I do know you, Phoebe and Rachel, will be received with great excitement. I'm sure in time you'll get used to the attention of the uncouth members of my court. And then if you don't pleasure them I'm sure I could obtain some of your younger siblings for their enjoyment. Don't look so shocked, it's what you people deserve. And better than what I should've done to you. I had planned a dismemberment. Yes, yes, I'm talking about killing you. But then I thought I might get a better outcome if I kept you alive." Her gown swished as she made her way back to her seat.

"Although, the thought of your bodies mutilated and hanging from trees does amuse me. Such a pity, but maybe we can have it both ways? Pleasure for the troops and murder. All fun and games, hey?"

The girls were shocked and shook with a deep fear, until finally with a snap of the Queen's fingers they were ushered out of the audience rooms and back to their gilded cages.

None of them had uttered a single word. As the doors closed behind them, they all started speaking at once.

"Cousin? Is she our cousin?"

"Did you see the trays of crystalized fruit? It was enough to choke a hippo."

"What did she want with us if she never lets us speak? Did she really mean all those threats?"

Phoebe gathered her sisters in a hug and while their heads were close together she whispered softly. "There might be listening devices in this room, so if we speak we need to use the air language from now on. As to Atalia being our cousin, well she is in a way. Her mother is my mother's cousin. Atalia is the result of a liaison with a French man and she never inherited the Air Whisperer talents we have. She's angry about this lack all her life, and no one can explain it, but the thought is some of the talents must come through our father's line." Pheobe brought her sisters closer with a brief hug. Needing the contact to feel strong herself.

"As to the amount of fruit, who knows why she's surrounded herself with so much. And lastly, I'm sure we'll be allowed or encouraged to speak at some stage, but always remember, we're not here as guests but rather as prisoners. She's evil. I can feel it to the tips of my toes. Our job is to return home in safety and as soon as we can."

The mantle of responsibility fell heavily on Phoebe's shoulders. Looking at her two younger sisters she had a yearning ache to step back into her carefree childhood. But the moment had passed and she must now accept this new role as leader. She tried to remember all she had learned over the years of being a child in her father's kraal.

Phoebe shook with anxiety, concerned all the Queen's threats would come to pass and she felt inadequate to the task of keeping them all safe. For now, the way ahead was fraught with danger and horror.

They spent the day checking out the escape routes from their accommodation. Their door was not locked but as soon as they exited, a guard was there to escort them. They could go to the gardens, but the first thing they noticed was the fine steel mesh which covered the area in a dome.

The guard snorted, "It is to stop the birds from eating the goldfish." He made a slurping noise as he eyed up the girls.

Maria pretended to trip and hurt her leg to distract the guard long enough for Phoebe to glide to the top of the trees and touch the mesh. It hummed with electricity and Phoebe returned to earth without detection by their escort. The walls around the garden were covered with mosaic murals to give the impression of the countryside. There were no gaps, no gates or windows to allow anyone to slip through and they went back inside with heavy hearts.

Their rooms were beautiful but for all they were cages to keep them under lock and key. Phoebe lay on the bed and soon her younger sisters joined her. They cried great gulping tears of fear. Maria and Rachel fell asleep, but Phoebe could not allow herself the luxury of relaxing.

No matter how much she thought and analysed she could see no way out. What if they were given to the troops to use as they saw fit. Phoebe dug her nails into her palms so hard a line of bleeding wounds appeared. The possibility of murder did not worry her. If it happened it happened, but smelly, rough men using her sisters was more than she could bear. Her imagination threw up scenes of debauchery and degradation made her soul quake. Should she sacrifice herself to the soldiers, but then there would be no guarantee the same fate would not await the younger siblings as time went on. No, another way had to be found. A surer, safer way.

CHAPTER ELEVEN

A clanging bell announced dinner and they were herded into the dining room by two guards. About one hundred people were seated around a large table made from a single span from a Guibourtia Tessmannii Bubinga tree.

Phoebe ran her hands over the highly polished surface. She had heard about this gift to the new king from a tribal leader in Nigeria. She remembered the excitement her father had shown to see this rare wood travel through their domain. He had almost cried to think another forest giant had died for man's vanity. He had spent a whole week walking through the Nkandla forests stroking the bark of all the ancient trees he could find. Talking to the forest and promising they would be unharmed. He returned happier to know his guardianship of the trees was not under any threat and his old friends were safe from the forester's axe.

Phoebe wondered how he felt now he was so far from his old stomping grounds and who knew what had been done to their precious forests in their absence.

At the top of the table sat the King of all the Zulus, who bore the incongruous name of Eric Shaka Dingaan. He was a surprise to the girls, they had believed him to be a monster of epic proportions. Large in statue and vicious in nature. Instead, they saw a young man of about twenty with sparkling white teeth visible through a wide smile lighting up his handsome face. His body was toned and covered in a crisply ironed white shirt tucked into blue jeans. Certainly nothing like their imaginations could have conjured up. Phoebe reminded herself Eric was their enemy and she should not be admiring his physique or his good looks.

Eric stood up at their entrance and sat when they did. He chatted to a man of similar age with the most piercing blue eyes they had ever seen. Then turned to them and smiled so Phoebe had to frown at her sisters who were smiling back at him.

"Welcome to my table, dear cousins. Mother tells me you've decided to visit us and become acquainted. This is a double pleasure for me. Firstly, to have more people my own age around me for a change and secondly to see what beautiful women you are. Now I need to get to know you each, so we can see if we have other things in common." He bowed low and the servants seated the girls on either side of the King. "Tell me your names and a little about yourselves to start with."

Phoebe sat with her hands folded neatly in her lap as she lifted her head and announced. "I'm Phoebe, daughter of Alpheus and Nyoni, Air Whisperer, lately from Nkandla and now residing on the plains of Ndlovu. I work with mechanical engineers for fun and milk cows for a job. I was brought here under duress and am desirous of returning to the bosom of my family." She smiled sweetly while looking directly in the eyes of Eric the King.

He was surprised at her frankness. "I'm sorry, Mother didn't tell me you were here by force. I'm sure it's a misunderstanding and will be sorted out as soon as possible."

Atalia laughed from the other end of the table. "Ah, my son, as your mother I sometimes have to do things for your benefit, and aren't always to your liking, but it's because I love you more than life itself. The girls will get to enjoy their time with us and soon ask to stay of their own free will and choice. I felt it was time you met with women of quality and character so you may find a wife. These three are the first of many and I'm sure other women will be flocking to the courts as soon as they hear what we've planned. A great dance for your twenty first birthday in two months' time." She nodded to the servants and the food was brought in on the heads of the many Zulus.

The meal did not allow for much conversation and once it was over, high kicking warriors put on a demonstration to the beat of the drum. Phoebe took the opportunity to look around at possible ways of escape, but there were guards on every door armed with assegai and even some with the dreaded Kalashnikov rifles.

Phoebe had practised changing into other objects over the past few months, but was still not able to shape shift for long periods of time. Her greatest gift so far was being able to manipulate the air to move things around. Rachel had started to find her talents and Maria at only eight was much too young to have any talents at all yet.

It would be difficult for Phoebe to get her two sisters out of the compound without detection. If talents with Air Whispering would not get them out then they would need to use their other guiles. Rachel offered to flirt with Eric to see if he could be persuaded to help. Maria would become friends with the guards and pretend innocence, all the while trying to find out possible escape routes.

Phoebe knew the King's court had an amazing engineering department and she would stay with what she knew best in the hopes of finding a way out, while at the same time giving her a few moments of peace in an otherwise difficult situation.

After breakfast the next morning, Maria put her little hand in the hand of the big guard and asked, "Is there anywhere I can play?" She batted her long eyelashes at him and he smiled.

Rachel asked various people where she might find the King and sat in his audience chambers listening to him act as judge to some minor dispute between tribal chiefs. Phoebe was hard at work at the forge and her beautiful silk dress was a mass of oil and smuts. She wore an apron to stop sparks from igniting her dress and found some hardy work boots to protect her feet, but the rest was forgotten as she found solace in the work of her hands and mind. It gave her an opportunity to think and assess her feelings for Eric. Was he really innocent in their abduction? And how did it change things? Shaking her head, she mumbled to herself, he was the enemy and not to be trusted.

The chief engineer kept a close watch on Phoebe, but after a while was satisfied she knew what she was doing and gave her the freedom to do as she pleased.

Later, Phoebe sat with the other workers and she listened to their conversations with interest. Atalia was the power behind the throne and it was her who decided what projects should have priority. Plenty of munitions and things connected to warfare were prioritized, and then a few projects on household items, but nothing with the finesse the Elephant people had developed. Their armour was chunky and heavy and inhibited movement rather than facilitate it. The chief engineer sat next to Phoebe.

"You know your way around a forge, my girl. Who did you train under because you're using practises I've not seen around here?"

"I studied under the master craftsmen of the Ndlovu tribe. I'm merely a novice compared to them and I've much to learn still. Your workshops here are well stocked with heavy machinery, but I don't see the tools for delicate pieces. Is there another facility to deals with them?" She smiled at the older man and saw his eyes crinkle as he smiled, but his gaze was steely and gave away nothing.

"Don't try to wheedle information from me, child. I've been commanded by the Queen to allow you to work here as long as you like, but you're still not to go outside these walls or gather information to be used against us in times of war." His smile grew wider and he winked at Phoebe with a hint of a sparkle in his eyes. "Don't underestimate the Queen and her plans for the future. She has eyes and ears everywhere and will know the moment you step out of line."

Raising her eyebrows in surprise, Phoebe gathered her tools and went back to work. Maybe the idea of using the engineers to help with their escape would not be as easy as she had imagined.

She found some sheets of brass and copper in a pile of discards and proceeded to form them into a beautiful statue. A flock of birds hovered in the air as a single child lay below with arm outstretched. It was very emotive and would remind the girls they were not alone.

By dinner time she finished the polishing of the piece. So delicate were the wings they were almost transparent. The bronze had been beaten and sanded, buffed and polished until each feather shimmered in the air.

Phoebe rushed to return to the rooms in time to change for the meal. Rachel and Maria brushed her hair and applied nail polish on toenails. Their hands moved as fast as the speed of light as they prepared their sister to meet company. The people at the dinner table were almost the same as the night before. Again, the food was exotic and rich and all three girls felt ill looking at it. They soon pushed their plates away and reached for the fruit and nuts they were used to.

A few extra chiefs were clustered around the Queen but the girls were again placed next to Eric the King. As they took their seats, Eric leaned forward, dipping his napkin in his glass of water and used it to remove a smudge of soot from the forehead of Phoebe. A thrill rushed through Phoebe's body as his hand brushed her cheek. She scowled at Eric but he was oblivious and tucked the napkin under his plate.

"My dear cousin, it looks like my Mother has put you to work in the steel mines."

Atalia laughed. "No, my dearest son, Phoebe enjoys the company of engineers. The chief engineer tells me she's created a most remarkable piece of sculpture. I've sent the servants to your room to collect it so we may all enjoy your skills."

Phoebe was shocked her day's activities had so speedily been reported to the Queen and sat back as her sculpture was placed on the table. Many of the people gasped in admiration and Eric stood up and peered at it closely.

"Remarkable. Ragnar, come and look, you'll appreciate this skill. Truly amazing. I wouldn't have imagined you could produce this in one day, or in fact one so young could be so skilled in creating such a beautiful piece of work. Congratulations, you've found something of interest here at the Royal Courts after all. When you didn't come with Rachel to the audience room, I was afraid I'd said something to offend you, dear cousin. Come, tell me more about the processes you employed."

Ragnar, the man with the clear blue eyes nodded his head as he looked at the statue. He smiled at her and winked in appreciation. Phoebe noticed quite a few people around the table were interested to hear what she had to say and it gave her a feeling of pride. She glanced up at Atalia and saw her cousin was not looking as impressed as the others. This did not suit her purposes. Phoebe should so easily have found her niche irritated the Queen.

Eric was still speaking and it took a moment or two for Phoebe to focus on what he asked. She answered his questions without any guile and by the end of the meal they were speaking as equals. He had no real knowledge of mechanical things but was interested to find out more. In fact, he was surprised to hear the workshops in the Royal Court were making weapons of war.

He raised his voice slightly. "Mother, did you know the workshops are building troop carriers and armaments?"

"Oh, of course, my dear boy. They're simply to make sure our citizens know they're safe in your domain." She was not pleased at all with Phoebe and her garrulous tongue.

Ragnar bent down and whispered in Eric's ear so quietly so none could hear what was uttered, but Phoebe could see they were very close friends and wondered at this strange pair and if they would be friend or foe at the end of the day.

When the girls returned to their rooms, Phoebe was quite excited. "Maybe we can become so much of an irritant to our dear cousin she'll simply send us home again. Wouldn't it be nice?"

But none of them really believed this would be possible. The threat of abuse was ever present.

Rachel and Maria wanted to hear all about the day with the engineers. The thrill of using such advanced tools and the abundance of precious metals had Phoebe pacing up and down as she spoke of the marvels of the workshop. Phoebe waxed lyrical until she noticed the stunned looks on her sister's faces. She asked them about their day and they told what had transpired. Rachel had become very bored listening to the king judge simple cases of land boundaries and cattle, but had pretended a fascination she did not feel. She realised this would not help in their bid for freedom and had wandered off in search of better things.

Maria had been taken to the kindergarten and had spent a happy day free from care.

"The climbing wall was amazing. It had a theme of the jungle and there were toy monkeys at the top of the wall. I asked the helpers to time me so I could improve my agility. I need to be able to climb to a safe place if I'm in danger."

Phoebe and Rachel felt the tears in their eyes as they imagined their little sister spending her day planning an escape plan of her own in case her big sisters were not there to help her in her hour of most desperate need.

"Enough doom and gloom girls. Today we decide to hope for the best and plan for the worst, but not to let us change who we are. Agreed?"

Rachel and Maria both nodded their heads in agreement with the hint of hope gleaming in their sad eyes.

CHAPTER TWELVE

After lunch Eric went to the gym for an hour and then another hour swimming laps in his private pool before sitting for a while with his secretary and a pile of papers. Rachel trailed after Ragnar and found out a bit more of his history.

Ragnar was the result of a week-long love affair his mother had with a visiting Norwegian sailor. He promised to return and save her from her life as a sex worker on the docks of Richards Bay, but it had been four years before he returned and sought them out. By this time Ragnar had been born with bright blue eyes and a shock of blond hair setting him apart from his siblings and other inhabitants of the township. He was teased by all and had only his mother to turn to for support and love.

By the end of a year, after giving birth, she had returned to her life as a prostitute on the docks and had become infected with the deadly African disease of AIDS. When his father returned Ragnar was excited and hoped things would become better. But after giving his mother a wad of money to help with bills, Ragnar senior had departed, never to be heard from again. His mother lived a few more years and then died. None of his older siblings wanted to take him in and the cash his father had left was not enough to significantly alter his life.

His refuge was the time he spent in the school-room. The day he turned ten, his safe place was also taken away from him and he was sent out to find work. He did odd jobs to support himself. But there were days when he earned nothing at all and went to his little cardboard box in the sugar cane fields aching with hunger. Some kind people did offer him a meal once or twice a week, but for a growing boy it was a drop in the bucket of need.

One day the King took Eric for a walk to encourage him to become more studious and stay away from the bad influence of his friends. He decided Eric needed a more balanced group of friends, especially those who valued learning.

"Dad they are my friends and I enjoy being with them." Eric smiled at his father.

At just that moment Ragnar stumbled onto the pathway as he tried to escape the teasing of his brothers and the king stopped him looking deep into his eyes. "This young boy will teach you how to appreciate learning."

Eric shrugged his shoulders but smiled shyly at Ragnar.

Ragnar responded to the largesse of the king by excelling in all he attempted. By the time Ragnar was fifteen years old, he had completed school and was sent on to university.

The king had taken pains to set aside a trust, funding Ragnar's academic requirements and leaving a tidy sum over for living expenses.

Rachel announced. "He is a very nice young man and it is possible he might help us escape."

"I don't think he could hurt anyone. He was very nice to me all day, even when I asked lots of questions. He likes numbers too and let me play on his computer. Phoebe he is the king's best friend and I am sure will be on our side if we want to leave."

Maria spoke of an almost empty playground. Only a few of the guards had children as the Queen did not encourage families within the compound. A vast hall filled with crafts and games was manned by two teachers who read them stories and guided them through the daily tasks. The other children were all familiar with each other and at first Maria had been ignored, but after one of the teachers asked her to introduce herself, she settled in fine.

"They asked me if I had any special skills or talents, so I did some bird song impersonations impressing them all. I spent most of the morning trying to teach Andre, one of the children of the chief of the guards, how to whistle. He said it was the best day ever and wanted to be my friend."

The girls laughed as they prepared for bed and Phoebe was glad their incarceration wasn't causing them any undue stress. They were really very adaptable girls and their parents would be pleased to see how they were coping. They had not seen any more signs of Thandi and worried she might have been prevented from entering the Royal Court through some device they were not aware of. All the girls knew their parents were doing everything in their power to free them and they needed to do their part.

Phoebe went to sleep dreaming of swimming in a large pool with tentacles trying to pull her down. As she thought she might drown, a hand pulled her up and she was safely ensconced in strong arms. When she looked up it was to see a grinning Eric bending closer to give her a kiss. She woke up with a gasp and it took her ages to fall back to sleep. She hoped she would not have the dream again as it had caused feelings she was not comfortable with. Nice feelings but inappropriate at this moment in time.

The following morning Rachel decided to see if the king's secretary could use a hand with the filing and basic office work or maybe she could spend time with Ragnar. Phoebe had found a stylish overall to wear to the workshops had been added to her wardrobe and Maria went off to see if Andre wanted to learn some more whistling tricks.

CHAPTER THIRTEEN

Alpheus and his wives were not far away from their daughters, but had no clue how to find their way into the impenetrable fortress faced them. Ndlovu and Izzie were both scouring the countryside to find animals to communicate with the animals inside the compound. Sipho and most of the younger children were still on the plains of Ndlovu and had the care of the cattle as their responsibility.

The three wives planned on visiting other Air Whisperer tribes to see if they could offer help. Alpheus was to remain at the kraal of his cousin and consolidate their attack plans. Their cousin had offered his home without any hesitation. He had felt the wrath of the Queen and had no love for the Zulu warriors who terrorized his young women as they worked in the fields.

Hemi, the cousin and his family, sent out scouts to see what they could find. Many of the guards lived in amongst the community and commuted to work on a daily basis. Hemi decided they would be the weakest link. He went off armed with a large pot of beer and visited a few of the guards pretending friendship as he acted the spy. A few beers under their belts and the men were more than delighted to share their thoughts about the Royal household.

No chink in the armour of the defences could be seen, no guard willing to take a bribe, no one with a secret able to be used against him. Hemi got the impression they were all scared of displeasing the Queen and even if they did not like what she was doing, they were not going to put their families at risk.

The days stretched out long for Alpheus as he worried about his precious children. Nyoni returned with news saying other Air Whisperers would back any play they would make. And were making their preparations to join them as soon as they could. Ndlovu came and reported the animals within the Royal Courts were unable to help as they were not free to move around.

Things looked bleak and Alpheus felt their options were limited and they would need to be patient and wait for the opportunity to present itself. It was Sarah who came up with the idea they could all enter the complex when the King had his coming of age ball in two months' time. This gave them time to work on a strategy and get word to the children inside the walls to be patient and not do anything impulsive.

The invites were being distributed to the chieftains to bring their most eligible daughters to the ball. A few people laughed at the ancient tactic of finding a bride for the King, but none of them wanted to miss out on the spectacle and sent in their acceptances. Even Alpheus received an invite and he was worried it might be a trap of some sort, but he sent in an acceptance.

Ndlovu offered to get his craftsmen working on a suit of armour for them each. It would appear to be fabric but could turn aside a blade or even a low calibre bullet. They went back to the Ndlovu plains and spent the next few weeks practising their fighting skills as well as their dance moves.

Extra security was put in place to protect the fortress while the adults were away.

Tembe was one of the young women invited to the ball and she worked with the engineers on sculpting jewellery hiding some nasty surprises. Earrings as listening devices and cameras. Necklaces and belts able to be employed as weapons of deadly destruction. Her bracelet was a marvel of ingenuity demonstrated to the family at dinner one night.

"Turn this jewel here and I can access a knock out drops putting a person to sleep in an instant. This clasp here is also a blow torch able to cut through a chain or lock in under a minute. But this is what I like the most, if you remove the bracelet it becomes a mini crossbow. Cool, isn't it?" She proudly twirled around with the pretty jewellery on her arm and then proceeded to show them what each finely crafted piece in the collection was able to change into.

Armour as thin as silk was brought for each of the women to wear and the men were dressed with coats and waistcoats no one would ever imagine were really woven steel threads. Nyoni wore gold with a necklace of fine diamonds, a bracelet of similar design and long drop earrings.

Thandi chose a fine silver dress and her jewels were all rubies including a belt of such perfection it would rival the best in the land. Sarah chose a steely grey colour with a muted palette of pale blue jewels including some vicious looking hair pins capable of doing some serious damage to an enemy. Izzie chose a green and gold dress floating around her as she moved.

Izzie twirled around the room and with a huff and a grunt Ndlovu joined her, dipping and moving around his wife.

He grabbed Tembe by one hand and the three of them danced smoothly over the floor to the enjoyment of their guests. For a moment, their troubles were forgotten. Tembe was not revealing to anyone her dress before it was time to prepare for the ball. No matter how much Sipho teased, or her own siblings cajoled, she would laugh and tell them to wait and see. She had not had as much fun as this for quite some time.

CHAPTER FOURTEEN

At the palace Phoebe picked up a bird song from her mother. It whispered to them. "Don't do anything silly until the rest of the tribe can help out." If this would lull the Queen into a sense of security she was delighted to comply. She lifted her face up in pleasure as the sweet clear birdsong washed over her. And she replied with her own song. Trilling her love for her parents and the joy she felt even though they were apart, knowing she was not alone.

Each morning she went off to the workshops and found something to do to keep her busy. She became friends with a few of the workmen. What she hadn't expected was Eric would take an interest in what she was up to. Each lunch time he would appear and bring with him a large meal to share with Phoebe. He would want to see what she was working on and then after about half an hour he would leave and her workmates would tease her she had an admirer and what was she doing getting her nails all dirty and chipped if she could lay around the pool with the King instead of working herself to the bone.

"Don't be silly, guys. Eric is being a good host and making sure I'm well looked after."

"Yeah, right. I saw the way he looked at you, girl. He showed more interest in you than in the food he ate. In fact, I think he might have liked a little nibble of you."

The workers all laughed, including the two women amongst them.

"Hey ladies, how about a bit of sisterly support here? The King isn't interested in me in a sexual way, is he?"

"Oh yeah, more than interested. He practically drooled over you and even with you having soot everywhere except where your safety glasses covered. I even saw his eyes wandering a little bit lower to peep at your twins."

The women laughed almost as much as the men did and Phoebe found herself blushing under her layer of soot. She knew they were only making fun of her, but the thought Eric might be interested in her was intriguing.

At dinner, she sat further down the table next to an aeronaut captain who flew one of the flying contraptions so beloved of the Zulu King. As she started chatting to him about thermals and air pockets she felt someone sit next to her on the other side.

The chair had previously been filled by a rotund chieftain from Swaziland, but when she glanced over, she saw he stood befuddled and bemused as the King gestured to him to take the head of the table.

"Eric, is there something you want to ask me?" asked Phoebe.

"No, I wanted to hear what was being discussed by Albert the aeronaut of course. Fascinating subject the control of an air ship."

"True, it's fascinating, so if you don't mind I would like to hear what Albert has to say."

She turned her back on Eric and was engrossed in technical terminology with Albert. Albert was a bit taken aback at her knowledge and interest, but as it was a subject he loved, he talked between mouthfuls of food. The King sat there quietly eating his food and smiled at the other people at the table. Phoebe could feel Eric's presence at her back and had to stop herself from turning to see what he was up to. Her spine tingled and at any moment she expected to feel his hand on her back. In fact, she hoped to feel his hand on her back, but it didn't eventuate and she was definitely disappointed.

Atalia let this behaviour ride for a few minutes and then pronounced, "Eric, enough of this silliness, be an adult and go and entertain your esteemed guests further down the table. Be a good boy. Mom knows best."

"But Mom, I'm quite content where I am and I'm sure I can learn a lot sitting right here."

With a big sigh the Queen proclaimed, "Eric I'm still Queen Regent for a few more weeks, so listen to me and do as you're asked to do." She flicked her ring encrusted hand at him and he finally got up and went and did as he had been instructed like a scolded schoolboy. Ragnar raised his eyebrows at his friend and they exchanged a smile.

He sat on the opposite side to Phoebe and every time she looked up he looked at her and would smile or wink at her as he chatted to his neighbours. As soon as dinner was over he was quick to ask her if she wanted a walk outside in the gardens. She felt her heart flip in her chest and a warmth grow in her whole body as if warm honey had been poured over her.

She replied yes to see what would happen and was surprised he took her outside the palace walls. Her heart fluttered as he entwined his fingers through hers. Her breath caught in her throat when he pulled her in front of him and tipped her chin up to the sky. He pointed out the stars above their heads as Phoebe fought the urge to rise into the air and make fly away from these feelings and the strictures of the Royal household. She thought of her little sisters still within the palace walls and decided to observe and perhaps see what Eric knew about their abduction.

"Eric, aren't you scared I'll fly off. I'm an Air Whisperer you know and can quite easily escape."

"Escape? But you're not prisoners. You're here to visit and learn from us. My Mom says you're to be kept safe, but she never informed me you were *prisoners*." He took her hand in his and she felt her knees grow weak as he led her to the side of the garden.

They sat on a bench as Phoebe spoke to him a bit about their kidnapping and interaction between them and the Royal troops.

"We're on our way to milk our cows when soldiers rose up out of the bushes and covered our noses with evil smelling rags. To be truthful we didn't feel scared for the moment as we thought it was a prank played by our brother. No time to tell our families, no time to say goodbye. Horrible Eric, absolutely terrible. It was when we woke up in the palace, it dawned on us our lives were in danger. The way the soldiers touched and looked at us still give us nightmares.

"Your Mother threatened, she wanted to murder us and put our bodies in trees for wild animals to devour or else to give us to the soldiers to use in any way they wanted. This is when we truly felt fear and wondered if we would ever get out of here in one piece. As the oldest sister I wanted to protect the younger ones, but I truly did not know if I was strong enough to do it on my own. We wonder if when we lie down to sleep at night if our lives will not change again for the worse."

She sighed deeply and had to swallow a lump in her throat as she remembered their fear.

"We imagine rough hands on our bodies and hot breaths on our cheeks and we wake up screaming each night, every night. Maria has asked we leave a light on so she might not be scared of the dark."

Phoebe stood up and paced backwards and forwards as she continued. She waved her hands in the air towards the heavens and then hung her head as she shrugged her shoulders in defeat.

"And this is a child who used to enjoy sitting out under the stars and watching for shooting meteors in the pitch-black night. Our lives were changed and not for the better the moment your Mother decided to kidnap us for her own ends. Rachel tries to be strong, but I hear her crying in the shower."

Phoebe tried to hold back the tears gathering on her lashes. Dashing them away, she continued.

"And it breaks my heart. Without hope, without anyone to turn and surrounded by strangers. We do not know who to trust. I doubt my own judgement of those I meet in case they turn on me. I hate this feeling Eric. I want to know the people around me are going to treat us with human kindness, and I no longer have a belief in this assurance."

Putting his arm around her shoulders in a gentle hug of comfort, Eric looked deep into her eyes and she felt the barriers of distrust crumble.

"No. You're mistaken. I'm King and I trust my Mother to help me learn my royal duties. I'm sure she doesn't know anything about what you're saying. Maybe there are some rogue troops who will need to be brought into line, but what you're talking about is a dictatorship."

He stood up and pulled Phoebe into his arms and lightly kissed the top of her head.

"Eric, how can you believe that the troops would go against your Mother and her goons? Have you not noticed the way people look at you? They are scared to death."

"My Dad taught me we have an obligation to look after the citizens of this great country, but never to abuse our power. My Mom knows this and she would be horrified if she heard what you're saying. Maybe we should go and tell her? She'll put your mind at rest. She's really a kind woman underneath her steely appearance. Come with me and we'll go and find her."

He took Phoebe by the hand and led her along the passages until they came to a large wooden door. The guard opened the door for them and they found Atalia behind a large desk with piles of papers in front of her. She frowned as she looked up and smiled at her son.

"Eric, what a great pleasure. And you brought Phoebe with you. Is there any reason for this visit? I'm busy with the plans for the ball and need to focus on the minute details required for the smooth running of this affair."

Phoebe caught a quick glimpse of some diagrams definitely not related to the ball, or at least she hoped not. They looked suspiciously like containment fields capable of trapping her family in an inescapable prison. She smiled sweetly as she stood in front of the desk.

Eric related to his mother all Phoebe had told him and they waited as Atalia took a large breath before she replied.

"Eric, my precious son, there are many in this land who would undermine your good works. Unfortunately, this has at times created problems amongst the populace requiring harsh retribution."

Tapping a finger lightly against her phone she continued.

"Phoebe's family chose to disobey a request and they did lose their home as punishment. I feel not all the children are to blame and I felt it would be beneficial to bring some of them here to re-educate them to a more harmonious outcome."

Atalia stood up and paced backwards and forwards as she pointed her hand at the young woman.

"Maybe in time, Phoebe and her sisters can help us subdue rebel elements in the boundaries of the land. If they could see the vision of a unified land, then they can benefit not only their own family, but all the people who are crying out for your protection. And yes, it could be Lesotho and maybe in time even Swaziland."

Eric's mouth had dropped open as he listened to his mother.

"This would greatly enhance our position in the land. Your Father would be so proud of you, Eric, if you could fulfil this dream of his. Power with kindness. Strength with compassion."

"Mother this isn't what Father would've wanted. I'm shocked this has been happening in the land I'm supposedly King of. What do the people think of me, Am I a monster? A tyrant? Recall the troops Mother. Immediately. We can re-assess our priorities."

"Oh no, I can't do it, Eric. I'm still Queen Regent for a while yet and I can achieve a lot in a few weeks. Trust me. I've every hope Alpheus and his wives will soon be under our power and will do our bidding."

Smiling smugly, she continued.

"They know we have their children and will find their allies aren't as supportive as they thought. I have plans for the greatest twenty first birthday gifts any king has ever had. The gift of a mountain kingdom on a plate. The plans are already in place and within a month the defences of Lesotho will crumble and melt like ice in the mid-summer sun."

She approached Eric and took his face in her hands and patted his cheeks lightly.

"It's for you I do this, my son. I'll be known as the Queen who delivered this marvellous treasure to you. I'll not be mocked anymore as the Air Whisperer who cannot fly. I'll be revered and honoured by you and by many of the weak and hapless chieftains of the land. I will have my moment in history."

Eric shrank away from his mother and the look of shock and horror on his face assured Phoebe he had known nothing of what had been happening. She took his hand and led him quietly out of the room as the Queen sat with her eyes closed as she envisioned her future glory.

Eric stumbled along the corridor and Phoebe led him into their rooms and seated him on a couch as she asked Maria to pour him a drink of orange juice.

"Here, Eric. Drink this. You received a shock and need to get your head around what you've heard."

It took him about five minutes before he looked up. "I'm sorry. I didn't know what was happening."

"Yes, we know. We thought it was you behind all the horrors we've witnessed, but we now know it was the work of your Mother."

"I need to go." Eric whispered as he stumbled out of the room drunk with shock. Phoebe felt sad it had been her who had opened his eyes to the atrocities, but maybe she was the best person for the job. At least she cared for him. As she thought this she blushed bright red and hoped her sisters would not notice.

The next morning the King did not come for his breakfast and the rumour was he had asked to go somewhere private to consult with a Sangoma. The girls looked at one another and with a raised eyebrow or two they went their own ways.

CHAPTER FIFTEEN

Rachel had to decide what to do with her day and decided to find her way to the kitchens and see if she could receive a cooking lesson or two.

Her mother, Thandi, had announced it was high time she was taught the art of creating tasty meals. At only fourteen, Rachel was not sure her mother was right, but it was a way to fill the day.

The chef was not amused and his eyes popped from his face as he struggled to control his anger.

"What's the meaning of this, mademoiselle? This kitchen is my domain and you can't wander in and disrupt the routine. Out, out, out."

Rachel was not intimidated as she smiled. "Oh, dear Chef, I have heard you're a great chef and I'm here to see if you have time to teach me one little thing a day. I'll stay out of the way, but I beg your indulgence. One little tiny trick of the trade and I'd be so very grateful."

"Mon dieu. I don't have time for this nonsense. One little thing could take the whole day to master. What's it you wish to learn to do? Sauces? Or maybe how to peel Madumbe?"

Some of the other cooks smirked quietly behind their hands and Rachel had to bite down on her rising temper. "Béchamel sauce. I'd like to learn to make your famous béchamel sauce, Chef."

Chef raised his hand to one of the lesser cooks and an apron flew through the air and landed in his hands. Another cook handed over a large wooden spoon and a third one a heavy bottomed saucepan.

"There, it's all you'll need for béchamel. Now go and let's see what you can already do. I'm not wasting my time with a total novice."

Rachel put on the apron and then tried to wrack her brains to remember how her mother made béchamel. The large cooking ranges were already hot, so all she needed to do was find a place to put the saucepan. A young girl handed her a block of butter and a jug of milk. Rachel soon had a roué of butter and flour cooking on the stove. She deftly added some salt and pepper and then some mustard powder to the mix. Finally, she added the milk and heard a tut, tut behind her as Chef shook his head in disgust.

"Lumps is what you're cooking, lumps. Susara come here. Susara is the pot girl and her job is to scrub the pots, so she is not even one of the lesser cooks, but I bet she could make a better job of this sauce than you have."

Susara was an albino girl of about the same age as Rachel and she lifted her watery blue eyes to Rachel and gave her a cheeky wink. "Warm the milk, Miss. You need to warm the milk, otherwise it will be lumpy."

"Excellent Susara, you may return to your true calling, getting the grime off those breakfast dishes. So there, Miss Rachel, you've learned the trick of the béchamel sauce. Now you can leave my kitchen and find something else to amuse you today. Go, go, out, out."

Rachel gaily stood at the kitchen door and waved her hand. "See you tomorrow Chef, I'll come and see what else you can teach me."

She found her way to where Maria played with her new friends and spent the morning making a batch of kinetic sand for the children to play with. She laughed with the other teachers, had children riding on her back like little monkeys and generally having fun. Rachel would one day be a beautiful woman and had a character drawing people to her like bees to honey. She had the ability to make people feel they were your close friends even after a short time.

Living in a large family with multiple mothers to guide her had taught her to compromise and negotiate. Nothing was worth arguing about, there was always another way of getting your way rather than screaming at each other. Her Mom called her the peace maker in the family and she liked the title very much.

At dinner the King was still not there and Phoebe became concerned the Queen might have found a way to restrain him so she could work unhindered at her evil plans. Maria went to talk to the guard who normally accompanied them and he informed them the King had definitely gone to the mountains to consult with the Sangoma, but there was an excessive number of soldiers who had accompanied them.

He said the Queen was worried about rebel factions in the country and wanted to ensure the King was kept safe. Phoebe was sure it was not to keep Eric safe and requiring so many soldiers to be deployed. What if the Queen planned some sort of abduction and then blamed it on the Suthu or even her own family of Air Whisperers? She had never felt as frustrated as she did at the moment. She couldn't leave the palace and there was no way of passing a message to her family.

Phoebe took Ragnar aside and he too was baffled at Eric's sudden decision to leave the palace. "Sorry, Miss Phoebe, he didn't confide in me. He was distracted last night when I popped into his room to say goodnight, but I know less than you do."

CHAPTER SIXTEEN

Outside on the plains Alpheus himself watched the soldiers as they marched the King further and further away from his palace. As they camped for the night Thandi would take a chance and infiltrate the encampment and see what she could find out. Her favourite form was always the rose petals, but tonight she chose to travel as the seeds of grass, landing at the feet of the King and listened.

"Captain Raz, we are getting further away from where the Sangoma has his kraal by the hour. Please explain."

"My King, your mother has instructed us you desired to travel your domain and see the great progress made during her regency. She's asked you open your eyes and in a day or two we'll take you to the Sangoma as promised."

"I'm the King and it's up to me to decide what I want to do, and what I want is to visit the Witchdoctor to consult with him as to the things I've heard. No more roaming the countryside. Tomorrow morning at first light we'll make our way to his kraal and from there I'll decide what and where we visit."

He rolled his karross around himself and lay down near the fire. Thandi whispered, "Eric, Eric. I'm the mother of Rachel. Please tell me if the girls are safe."

He sat up with a jerk and frowned at the ground where the voice had emanated from. He had never come into contact with her type of talents before and so in front of his eyes she subtly changed into the fragrant rose petals she so enjoyed portraying. One little petal rose up and landed on his forearm and slowly stroked him. Another petal landed on his shoulder. "Don't be afraid. This is one form the Air

Whisperers can take. I don't mean you any harm, I wish to know what has happened to our girls."

Lying down again Eric proceeded to whisper the story of the past weeks. Of Phoebe's skill, of Rachel and her sweet spirit and even Maria and her teaching the children to whistle. Then he spoke of his Mother and what she had done and what she still planned to do. He recounted his shock at the betrayal of all he believed in and all his Father had wanted for the kingdom.

Captain Raz paced the camp site and as he approached, Eric pretended to be asleep and mumbled in his sleep. Captain Raz stood quietly for a moment trying to decide if Eric was really talking in his sleep or something else, but finally he moved on. It was late in the night when Thandi finally left the camp site and flew home to her family to report.

CHAPTER SEVENTEEN

Xele, Isifunda and Bala stepped forward to offer their skills once they heard the plans. Sipho and Tembe wanted to come along on any skirmish with the soldiers, but Nyoni stood up and shook her head.

"Yes, you may all come along, but remember it's the King we're dealing with here and there might be long term consequences if we make a mistake."

Alpheus suggested they all get a good night's rest as the next day they were going to see how they could help the King and perhaps find a way to free the girls from the palace. No one really expected to sleep after the excitement of the meeting, but soon snores could be heard across the plains.

At first light Izzie gathered them all together and gave instructions to those who were to stay and those who would accompany the group. The women of the Air Whisperers were sent ahead and Xele, Isifunda and Bala changed into pachyderms and carried supplies on specially designed panniers.

They led the group at a steady lop eating up the miles without straining the runners. They stopped for a quick bite to eat at midday and by mid-afternoon they could see the Zulu warriors ahead at the bottom of a valley.

The King was injured as he limped quite badly and slowing the progress of the warriors. They tried to push him along, but every few steps he would demand a seat for a moment, rubbing his ankle.

"Okay, people. I think the King is pretending to be injured to give us time to get into position. The road they're taking leads through a valley with steep cliffs on either side,

I suggest we all set ourselves up there. Xele and Bala, I want you two, in your human forms, to pretend to be peasants working in the field over there."

Izzie pointed her finger at a partially worked field to the right. "When the soldiers approach I want you to ask them if they have something to eat as you are hungry. Try to get close to the King. Thandi and Nyoni can you get as close as possible to help in any way you can. Ndlovu, Alpheus and I'll stay out of sight, unless we see a need for force. But the whole exercise should be kept as low key as possible. Everyone understand?" She said as she surveyed the intent looks on their faces.

"Fine let us go."

Isifunda, Tembe and Sipho cut off any chance of retreat and happily went off on their errand laughing and talking together.

CHAPTER EIGHTEEN

The King noticed the gully ahead with its steep sides and hoped it was where the ambush would be held. He gathered himself up and hobbled forward calling. "Captain Baz, I'm feeling much better. Perhaps we can take an extended break once we reach the shelter of those cliffs ahead?"

Captain Baz was happy to comply. He was sick and tired of the weak and injured King and his warriors' grumbles. Two workers in the field called out to him for food. He beckoned them closer. "If you want food you lazy peasants, you can work for it. Pick up the King between you and jog as fast as you can to the bottom of the cliffs and then I'll reward you with food."

"Of course, great Zulu warrior, it'll be our pleasure." Linking arms, they formed a seat and the King was comfortably ensconced on their strong arms. They jogged at a gentle pace and Xele managed to whisper to the King.

"We're with the Ndlovu people and are here to help."

As they approached the cliffs they saw a troop of baboons wandering the rocks. The largest male put on a show of defiance. The Zulu warriors took out their Kalashnikov rifles and were about to take pot shots at the apes when the King stood up. "Lower your guns."

They did not know whether they should take orders from their King or their Captain and glanced towards Captain Baz in confusion.

"My King, what's the problem with the men blowing off a bit of steam by improving their targeting skills? Surely a few shots will be acceptable?"

"Captain, do you really want to alert any potential enemies to our position. You're after all protecting the King of the Zulus, are you not?"

Xele and Bala stood behind the King with their arms at their sides and silly grins on their faces. When Captain Baz noticed them, he told his men. "Make a fire, men, put on a pot for some herbal tea." They heard singing and laughing coming along the road and could see three young people walking towards them. "Oh, for goodness sake, it's like we're about to have a party, put some meat on a grill while you're at it, we might as well make it a feast." grumbled the Captain.

Eric laughed and spoke to the new guests. The Captain and his soldiers took themselves off to the far side of the pathway to drink their tea and chew on the tough chunks of meat they had charred on the grill. One of the warriors disappeared behind a bush to relieve himself and was silently whisked away by Thandi and Nyoni.

As each of the warriors followed their lead, the men were relieved of their guns and taken to tree tops over the hillside. Captain Baz lazed against a rock with his eyes half closed and oblivious to what had transpired with his men. Finally, it was only him and a single soldier.

When Bala and Xele walked towards them and smiling slightly, they overpowered them and disarmed them in the twinkling of an eye.

The King was miraculously cured of his ankle injury and happy to take a little trip with his new friends. The whole rescue had gone off without a hitch.

Nyoni turned into a Lammergeyer and grasped the King by his shoulders flew him to the Elephants fortress on the plains. The rest of the group arrived after nightfall to find the King sitting around a campfire. He chatted to the children and told them fantastical stories entrancing them all. He spoke of the fire breathers who could roast a chicken from fifty paces and how they held flames in their hands without getting burned.

They gasped as he recalled riding on the back of dolphins in the sea off Mtunzini. Riding the waves far out to sea and watching great whales jump out of the sea as if on wings. Of Eagles only living in one place in Zululand and lived amongst the raffia palms. How monkeys leapt from trees high in the forests without fear, but when they saw a snake they would faint right away and fall out of the forest canopy with a great crash. How turtles returned to the very same beach from whence they themselves had been hatched, even though they had never returned for many years. But somehow, they knew the way back no matter where they travelled in the whole wide oceans of the world. A few of the children dropped off to sleep, but many of the older ones and even the adults sat fascinated until the stars themselves dimmed in the sky.

The warriors were in a prison formed from thorn bushes and woven vines and were unable to escape. They were fed and given things to sleep on, but there were no luxuries and even though they were unhappy to be captured, they were comfortable enough.

At first light Thandi went to find the Sangoma and ask him to join them at the fortress. In the meantime, Nyoni spent time with the King, talking quietly, away from the others.

Izzie asked Alpheus what his wife was doing and he shrugged. "My wives do things and they don't include me and I'm happy that way. I trust them implicitly and know they have our best interests at heart. If Nyoni wants to tell us what's happening, she will in her own time."

Eric gave Nyoni a hug at the end of their talk and then went to sit next to the lake and looked off into the sky deep in thought. He didn't join them all for lunch and his demeanour kept even the most boisterous child away from him as he continued to brood.

As the sun set Eric finally joined the families around the camp fire for dinner. He never uttered a word to anyone all night and everyone gave him space to think. Some of the children wanted to hear more of his stories, but a hard look from the parents quietened them down.

The next morning the Sangoma arrived and Eric was busy in a meeting with the witchdoctor until well after lunch. The Witchdoctor then joined the families for a meeting to see if there was anything he could help them with. Various members of the families came forward to ask questions.

Aliki had a persistent infection he was concerned about. Malia wanted something to remove blemishes from her skin and Tatia wanted a tonic to help her with her schoolwork. They were each given a solution to their issues and went away happy.

Once the business had been dealt with the families put on a talent evening of amazing skills to entertain the two visitors. Young men danced and jumped in the flickering fire light, girls twirled and flipped through gymnastics. Nyoni, Thandi and Sarah used their voices to sing songs bringing tears to the eyes. Ndlovu showed feats of strength, lifting more than his body weight above his head, both in his human and elephant forms.

Alpheus and Sipho put on a show of mock battle using knobkerries and had many of the younger men eager to join in. Finally, the children were sent to bed and the adults could talk.

Eric informed them it was time he returned home to see what could be salvaged from his Mother and her machinations. The Sangoma agreed to accompany him and the Air Whisperers planned to move closer to the Palace in time for the ball, so they would not be far behind. Bala, Xele and Isifunda would be a guard of honour for Eric and cement their allegiance with the King.

Farewells were shared as the men would be leaving before dawn to give them the chance of getting to the palace before nightfall. When Eric got to the gates of his palace his mother was waiting and demanded to know where Captain Baz and his men were. "They decided to visit some outlying districts on their own and become acquainted with the citizens of this great country. They'll not be back for some time, if ever. How have you been, dear Mother? Well, I hope?"

He said nonchalantly as he walked past her. "I'm tired and hungry, please arrange for my companions to be fed and accommodated for the night. Thank you and good night, I'm off to bed."

Atalia stood with her mouth slightly open. Her son had never spoken to her with such authority before and she was nonplussed for a moment. "Wait a moment, my boy. I need more of an explanation. Where have you been and who are these men? I demand an answer."

"Demand away, Mother, but I'm too tired to reply. Know the men are my friends and I'll hold you accountable for their wellbeing. As to where I've been. I've been having my eyes opened. And now I really must rest. I've much to do before my coming of age, Madam. Goodnight."

CHAPTER NINETEEN

The next morning Eric was out early and didn't stop for breakfast before going out with the troops and working on hand to hand tactics for a few hours. He wanted some stick fighting to be taught and not only the violent gun and knife skills.

An old man from a nearby village was summoned and herd boys were sent out with axes to cut down some suitable sized sticks to be used by the soldiers. Hemi was one of the chosen tutors of the stick fighting and showed the men the way to parry and thrust and how to protect their vital organs against the enemy.

By lunch time the soldiers were bruised and aching. The King was happy with their progress and grabbed a picnic basket before going to the forge to see how Phoebe was doing. Her work mates winked at her suggestively and she admitted she had missed Eric and his attention. She could not stop herself smiling at him and tried to stop the frantic beating of her heart without success.

Quietly between mouthfuls of delicious delicacies he informed her where he had been and what had been happening. He saw the tears well up in her eyes as he spoke about her family and quickly started telling a joke so she could deal with them before her compatriots noticed.

"A florist went to a barber for a haircut. When it came time to pay for the service his money was refused as the barber said he was doing community service and the haircut was free. The next morning the barber found a thank you note and a bunch of roses on his doorstep. Then a policeman had his haircut and was told the same. The following morning, he presented a tray of doughnuts to the barber with many thanks for his skills. The next to receive a free haircut was a royal courtier. The following morning there was no thank you note, but there were another ten courtiers saying, 'We heard there were free haircuts available.'"

Phoebe laughed at the feeble joke and wiped away the errant tears.

"Your mother revealed to me some interesting facts about the Royal family. I'm still trying to deal with the new information. Maybe we can meet after dinner tonight and talk some more?" Eric whispered in her ear, causing a shiver to race through her body, before picking up the empty basket and going about his daily duties.

Phoebe worked quietly on a new piece of sculpture all afternoon and as she stood back and surveyed her work she was surprised at how much it represented her feelings. She was quite embarrassed and wondered if others could see what she could.

Rachel came into the workshop and stood next to her sister. "Wow. A love story if ever I saw one. Bodies entwined with nothing left to the imagination. Fabulous movement. I don't know if you want the Queen to see this one? She might lock you in a dungeon or something."

Tanya, Mya and Trevor from the workshop floor came over and stood looking at it from every angle.

"Do you have a dirty little secret, Phoebe? Have we missed something or is it still in your imagination?" The engineers laughed and went off to their respective homes as Phoebe stood blushing next to her latest creation.

The chief engineer had heard the ribald comments and came over for his own look. "Good engineering skills, girl. Are there any kinetic elements? Let's see then."

Phoebe touched one rhythmic curve and the two figures moved into something quite different as it metamorphosed into two birds flying with wings touching.

"Mmm, maybe we should leave it in this stage for the moment, Phoebe. I'll not report this to the Queen. I'll tell her you're working on a piece representing movement." He winked at the two girls and went to change into his street clothes.

Phoebe held her breath and slowly let it out as she realized she had been apprehensive as to how it would be reported. She had not consciously made the erotic sculpture, it had developed on its own from her sub-conscious. Tucking it into her backpack, she went with Rachel to find Maria and go to their rooms for a quiet moment before it was time to dress for dinner.

Phoebe told them about Eric and his visit to their families and Maria sobbed as she admitted to missing her Mom and siblings.

"I dream of Mom every night and she's always crying. I want to hug her until all the hurt goes away. Will we see them soon? It feels like forever since we were taken away from them. Dad is in my dreams too, but he stands and smiles at me and before I wake up he blows me a kiss like he always does when he tucks us up in bed each night. Can't we do something? Anything? I try to be cheerful but my heart inside feels sick all the time."

The three girls sat in a huddle and all three cried as they admitted to being homesick. "I'm the eldest and I should be old enough not to need my Mom, but I miss her every day, Maria. Every morning when I wake up, I want to see her face and every night I wish I could tell her things about my day. I work so hard at my engineering because it helps me to forget where I am."

Wiping tears from her cheeks she admitted.

"I miss Dad too. I love when we go for walks in the fields and tells me the stories of the trees and he can name them all. He spoke of the jumping beans in the Tamboti tree's beans. I loved it when he put the beans in our hands and waited for them to move. He would laugh and laugh when we yelled in surprise. Such good memories. Mom taking me to the top of trees and allowing me to swing on the branches high above the world. I can't wait to get back to them so I can tell them how much I love them all."

Rachel didn't say anything for a moment and then added her lament to her sisters. "I keep smiling by thinking it's one less day until I see Mom and Dad again. I feel the petals in the gardens and imagine they are Thandi, in her petal form and sometimes I speak to them as if they are her. I think we're all coping in our own ways. But it won't be for much longer. The ball is only a few weeks away and I'm sure we'll be free after the party."

None of them felt much like a formal dinner at night and sent a message they were unwell and wished to eat in their rooms. They dressed in their pyjamas and collected ingredients for face masks and polish for their nails. They combed each other's hair and added beads to the braids. The servants brought them a simple meal of pizza and fruit salad for dessert.

Phoebe had forgotten she had made a date with Eric to meet him after dinner, but when he knocked at the door to ask how they were feeling, she whispered she would see him tomorrow as tonight was for her sisters. He touched her cheek gently. "I understand."

"I have something to give you Eric, hold on a second and I'll get it for you."

Phoebe handed him the wrapped sculpture she had completed during the day and quietly closed the door on him. Tonight, was family night and even though she would like Eric to be part of her family, now was not the time.

Early the next morning the girls were woken by blasting trumpets and pounding drums. They threw some clothes on and rushed out into the corridor to see what was wrong. The guards were not guarding their door and they were able to run outside to where the rest of the Royal court gathered in various stages of dressing.

A span of oxen pulled a strange wagon contraption floating above the dusty road. Flags flew and soldiers marched at the rear and front of this spectacle. Atalia and Eric stood in the middle of the crowd and as the wagon stopped, they stepped forward and greeted the guests.

First a beautiful woman flew out of the wagon and threw herself at Eric, wrapping her legs around his waist as she kissed him all over his face and neck in a frenzy of affection.

"Eric, oh, poor man. When I heard you only had Ragman and a grease monkey to keep you company, I insisted Dad and Mom arrive early for the ball so I could keep you company."

He wasn't interested in detaching her from his torso and he laughed back into her face. "Namaqua, you saucy minx. You can let me take a breath or two now." He placed her on her feet and then continued. "What've you been up to since we met? Breaking the hearts of all the young men in New York and Paris? You look stunning. It obviously agrees with you."

A handsome man leaned against the side of the wagon, watching this whole display with interest. Eric turned to him and hugged him. "Per, it's good to see you man. It's been too long. Let me welcome the rest of our visitors and we can spend some time catching up on your life."

A large rotund woman managed to swing her legs over the side of the wagon. A tall step ladder was brought forward and she descended gracefully. She stood on the driveway and carefully smoothed her dress down around her massive hips. She wore a large hat on her head and her neck was encircled with so many jewels the flesh between the gold and diamonds was barely visible.

From the other side of the wagon a man who appeared who was even larger than the woman. He wore a golden ring around his forehead, thick as a man's wrist, but because of his large bulk it looked like a delicate circlet.

Atalia approached and bowed low to the couple. "Nkomo, Nyama, what a pleasure you could come early for the celebrations. Come inside and I'll have some sustenance brought for you. I'm sure you're fatigued from your long journey."

The Queen led the way into the dining room and the girls found themselves swept along with the crowds. People whispered, Nkomo was the largest cattle baron in Africa and was rich beyond anyone's imaginings. Nyama was his senior wife and the mother of the beautiful Namaqua. Nyama had been the beauty of Africa in her day, and had managed to capture the attention of Nkomo who had whisked her away from the fleshpots of Europe to give her a home to rival any palace or castle in the world.

They owned their own private jet as neither of them could fit on a commercial airline, even in the first-class seats. Boeing had been tasked with creating a jet plane capable of accommodating their great bulk as well as their courtiers and band members. And it was a vehicle of opulence costing an arm and many a leg.

Namaqua sat on Eric's lap as the rest of the company found their seats. He had a strange look on his face and Phoebe decided it was better if their family sat further along the table. She could not quite convince herself to eat in their rooms, like an animal being mesmerized by a snake, she could not take her eyes off the two people at the top of the table. She ate her plate of omelette and toast as if in a dream. Sipping her freshly squeezed orange juice while never taking her eyes off Eric. Anxious for the least little bit of reassurance he had not forgotten her. Finally, she shook herself out of her funk. He had every right to spend time with his friends and she reminded herself he had said nothing about wanting to be exclusive or even anything special between them. This was no time to be jealous she reminded herself.

He was a bit embarrassed and tried to get Namaqua to sit on her own seat, but she was not having a bar of it, laughing and giggling each time he shifted. A quick glance at Atalia showed a smug smile all over her face.

Per sat with his legs akimbo, around the back of a chair, picking at his food with his long fingers. Ragnar walked into the room and Per sat up like a hound spotting a hare to be chased. "Rag Tag. Is that really you? Are you still hanging around the table of the king waiting for scraps? You should be ashamed of yourself. Being a parasite is never a good look, Raggie."

"Oh, you can talk Per. You've never done a day's work in your life and if my father hadn't given you an allowance, you would be begging for food like any wild dog in Zululand." laughed Namaqua.

Ragnar quickly took a few items of food off the buffet and with a smile and nod to the girls and Eric, made his escape while Namaqua made fun of Per until even Eric looked irritated with his guest.

With breakfast over, Phoebe went quietly to the workshops and spent the day designing various projects and then discarding them. No one disturbed her and when at lunchtime there was no King to bring a picnic lunch for her, her workmates happily shared their sandwiches with her.

Someone whispered to her Eric and his friends had used the four-wheeler bikes and taken off into the hills for the day. She could not settle to her work all day and realised she was showing the signs of jealousy. Angry with herself for being such an air headed romantic, she fiddled with odds and ends until even her supervisor was getting fed up with her. She wasn't happy with any of her creations and threw the drawings in the bin at the conclusion of the work day. Hands in pocket, head down she stalked off without saying a word.

The chief engineer waited for her to walk outside before dipping his hand in and retrieving the plans. A few of the other workers came to look at what had been discarded and Mya put her hand forward. "Can I try my hand at one of those Chief?"

He nodded and each of the blueprints had been taken by the workers for their own personal project in honour of Phoebe.

CHAPTER TWENTY

Dinner was a repeat of breakfast with Namaqua and Per talking loudly and drinking copious amounts of alcohol as they laughed about their day's antics. Phoebe looked up through her eyelashes at Eric and saw him looking at her with a strange look in his eyes. As the meal came to an end a servant slipped a note into Phoebe's hand.

It was written by Eric. *"Sorry I missed lunch. Can I meet you later in your rooms? I will come alone."*

She looked up and nodded at Eric with a small smile. When dinner was over the Queen clapped her hands and a live band appeared and played music. Namaqua grabbed Eric by the hand and pulled him onto the dance floor. Per looked around and spied Rachel. He didn't even ask for her permission, but pulled her roughly onto the floor and twirled her around.

She was bemused, but had no way of escaping without causing a scene. Many of the older people left and only the courtiers and their wives who were young enough to enjoy the music were left to dance.

Phoebe took Maria off to bed and as soon as she was settled, she returned to make sure Rachel got back to their rooms safely.

Per had grown tired of the young woman and now danced suggestively with a married courtier. Her husband stood in the doorway scowling in disgust. The wife looked like a stunned mullet as she tried to keep Per at a distance, not wanting to offend a special guest of the king.

Ragnar was nowhere to be seen and Eric sat and watched the dancing with Namaqua draped over him like a feather boa.

Rachel and Phoebe were able to sneak out and get back to their rooms without any problem. Rachel too turned in for bed and Phoebe stayed up waiting for Eric. She nodded off to sleep when she was woken by a soft tap on the door.

"Phoebe, Phoebe are you awake? Can I come in?"

Phoebe quickly went into the corridor so they did not wake the girls. "Eric it's late and my sisters are asleep. Can we go into the gardens perhaps to talk?"

He took her hand and they ran through the dimly lit corridor and into the garden. Phoebe felt her heart lift in joy and had to stop herself smiling like a silly loon in happiness.

"Phoebe, I need to tell you what your mother told me first and then maybe the rest will make sense. Firstly, Nyoni informed me the Royal line has a special talent has been kept secret all these years. My Father never shared the knowledge with me, but I have felt the stirrings of this gift over the past few months. It's the gift of discernment. I have to touch someone to feel what they're really thinking. People can tell me anything they like, but when I touch them I can see through any subterfuge. A handshake, a pat on the back, anything, and your Mom tells me in the future I might only have to look at someone to know what they believe.

"Today, when Namaqua jumped onto me, I knew about all the things she tried to hide from me. The cheating, the lies, and the way she wanted to use me to hurt others. I thought she was my friend, but she's closer to being my enemy.

"Then Per gave me a hug and I felt his anger and hate like a black cloud. He is envious of my wealth and power. I didn't want to spend a minute with either of them, but had no idea how to get out of it without them finding out about my talent.

"With you, Phoebe, I feel sunshine and love, compassion and caring, intelligence and wisdom. I can't tell you why I didn't tell you all this before. I am an idiot and beg your forgiveness. I'm not worthy of you and want to know anything I've done to hurt you has been done because I'm not as brave as you. Do you forgive me?"

Phoebe realised she held her breath while he spoke and she now felt light headed. Throwing her arms around his neck she never uttered a word as she snuggled in tight to his side. They spent the whole night talking and touching each other. Neither of them wanted to sleep or separate for any reason. Any thought of sleep vanished from their minds.

As the sun rose above the horizon Eric and Phoebe quietly slipped back into the girls' room. Rachel and Maria were awake and rubbed the sleep out of their eyes, they came over to give him a hug. Eric called a servant and ordered hot chocolate drinks with French toast to carry them through to breakfast. The four of them sat on the floor licking syrup from their fingers as Phoebe and Eric told them what had happened during the night.

Eric looked over at Rachel. "When you hugged me, I could see right into your soul. No, it's not something bad. I promise you, your parents can be proud of the marvellous daughter they've raised. Peace and bravery, innovation and imagination floats around you. I can feel your love for your family shimmering off you like a sheet of silver."

Rachel smiled in delight as Eric turned to their youngest sister.

"Maria, you too have a beautiful spirit. I can see one day you'll be an example to everyone around you. You'll able to read something and retain the information. This is an uncommon skill. What you have, my sweet child, is a beauty inside and out. Thank you for giving your love so freely to all those around you."

Eric spread his arms wide as if trying to show how great her love was in a finite way.

"You never let others push you into being mean and nasty. My dear you'll be a great shining light in this world of ours one of these days. Never change." He kissed her on the forehead. Maria blushed a pretty pink and put her chubby little hands to her cheeks as she lifted her chin and pulled her shoulders back.

Eric left to attend to some duties and the girls floated on a cloud of happiness as they prepared themselves for the day.

When they finally wandered into the dining room Atalia happily surveyed her son and his friends. "I hope you have some plans today, Eric, my liege, including some fun with your friends. A trip to the city and a night out on the town? A picnic at the beach maybe? Namaqua my dear, what's your wish. I'm sure Eric will be more than happy to give you your every desire."

"Oh Atalia, I think we'll take Daddy's plane and go to Paris for the night. It will be fun, Eric. Daddy won't mind, will you, Daddykins?" There was no place on her father's lap for her to sit, but she managed somehow to drape herself over his bulk. "And your credit card, Daddy. A girl has to have a bit of spending money." She kissed her father on his cheek while extracting the card from his wallet.

He muttered something about never having used the credit card himself but both his wives and his children had worn it out with overuse.

"Oh Daddy, don't be a grump. We'll see you tomorrow or maybe even the day after. Come Per, Eric lets go then. We can buy anything we need as we go, we don't need to pack a thing." Eric shrugged in resignation and followed the others out of the room with a glance behind as if looking for an escape route. He stopped and had a quick chat to Ragnar in the passage and then continued on.

The girls came back from their various activities to find they had been moved to a much smaller room underground. It was very much like a dungeon but without the chains to keep them tied down.

Atalia sent one of her courtiers to explain the palace expected an influx of visitors and if their parents were not prepared to be accommodating as to the Queen's wishes, then the girls would have to pay the price by having less luxury.

Phoebe smiled at the woman. "Tell the Queen we thank her for her hospitality and are happy to be moved to a smaller suite of rooms."

Once the woman had left Rachel asked, "Are you nuts? Why did you thank the Queen? She's a witch and evil to boot."

"Ah, little sister, it's all a mind game with Atalia. She wants us to be depressed and down trodden, but if we act calm and contented she won't know what to make of us. I like to keep her guessing. It's a harmless form of fun and really, we don't need fancy rooms. We are prisoners no matter where we sleep. I think she was waiting for Eric to leave before starting her plans. I wonder what else she'll get up to while he is away."

The girls put on smiley faces around the dinner table and noticed every so often Atalia would frown in their direction. She valued fine furnishings and trimmings so much she thought it was a punishment to be denied a pretty room. Phoebe flirted with the aeronaut and Rachel leaned in close to hear the mumbled words of Nyama, the beef baron's wife.

Maria pushed vegetables around her plate in boredom as the hum of conversation lulled her. They did not stay for the evening's entertainment. This night it was the turn of the gymnasts and a team of cheerleaders threw each other in the air with great skill.

Their new rooms were close to the diesel generator and all night the great machine made strange noises, keeping on waking them up. None of them slept well and were bleary eyed at breakfast

Atalia's lady in waiting came up to them. "You can't go about your normal daily activities. You're to return to their rooms for the day. Now."

Phoebe got up and hugged the woman much to the courtier's surprise. "Oh, tell the Queen thank you so much. Ever so kind of her to notice we needed a day in bed. How gracious she is. Can I go and give her a hug? Please."

The courtier backed away in horror and stammered a negative answer saying Atalia was very busy with dignitaries. The girls smiled happily as they skipped down the passage towards their mean little rooms. They had collected some fruit from the breakfast table on their way out and were well stocked in case they were denied lunch.

Ragnar followed them and assured them when Eric returned all would be restored. He filched a basket of muffins for them to snack on during the day.

The Chief engineer was shocked Phoebe was not at her workstation. She worked harder than most of his normal staff and some of them needed guidance on the plans Phoebe had discarded. He sent a message to ask Phoebe's whereabouts and was informed Phoebe was detained indefinitely along with her sisters.

He gathered his team of engineers together and spoke about the news. None of them were happy because they all admired Phoebe and her skills and enjoyed her company and sense of humour. Many of them went home and told their families and friends about the gentle girls kept prisoner in the palace and the news went like wild fire around the countryside.

It did not take long for Alpheus to hear about it and become concerned. A strange group of people gathered at the home of Hemi after dark. The Chief Engineer, a few of the guards and the teachers huddled together and whispered their distress. The Chief thought the Queen was trying to force the Air Whisperers to concede to her demands and the teachers had tears in their eyes as they imagined their friends being subjected to this tyranny. But at the end of the evening none of them had any idea how to free the girls. They would all go away and think about it and hopefully come back with a plan the next night.

Alpheus and Hemi looked at each other when the others left. Hemi pulled a notebook towards himself and made two columns. Pros and cons were the titles, but after a few minutes there were only cons and not many pros. They needed inside help.

The three guards would be a help, but were greatly outnumbered by those backing the Queen and her play.

PART THREE
OLD ENEMIES

CHAPTER TWENTY ONE

The following day stretched long for everyone. The girls were allowed out into the garden for a short time at dawn and dusk. Their food was brought to them on trays. The air conditioner switched off and the room became dank and overheated. They wet clothes and draped them over their heads and switched on the fans in an effort to cool off.

Ragnar brought them some fans to use and a box of books and art supplies to keep them amused. At lunch time Chef sent a minion down to smuggle in some ice cream and fresh fruit for the beleaguered girls.

What they did not know was there were many planning their escape. The engineers hoped to short circuit the mesh above the garden and find a way of opening it up for the girls to float through. The teachers were prepared to act as decoys and dressed to resemble the girls. They would make a feint through the halls of the palace and hopefully lead the guards in the opposite direction.

The three guards prepared to help in this endeavour managed to get themselves rostered on as their personal guards for the day. The note came with their dinner to say they should prepare themselves for their escape attempt at midnight.

It was a new moon and outside was dark as pitch. The girls found some dark coloured clothing and waited quietly in their rooms. At midnight, they listened to the chiming of the great clock and waited. But no one came. Finally, they all fell asleep in exhaustion.

At about three in the morning a large hand shook the girls awake and they sleepily followed the guard into the garden. Standing in the centre were their two mothers waiting to help in any way they could.

They rushed forward and hugged their parents and were about ready to fly out of their cage when lights were switched on and they found themselves in the glare of spotlights. Men stood up amongst the plants with guns pointed right at the family reunion.

"Did you think I wouldn't hear about this stupid stunt, my dear niece?" Atalia stepped forward and gloated at seeing her relatives standing helpless before her.

Nyoni placed her daughters behind her and stepped forward "Of course not, my dear aunt, we knew you have ears everywhere and depended on you showing your hand so decisively."

The lights were switched off and the garden was plunged into darkness. A guard started shooting where moments before he had seen the family.

"Stop idiots, stop shooting. You'll hit our own men." Yelled the Captain of the guards. "Someone get the light working."

Atalia was furious as she saw her plan had backfired so dramatically. There were three guards nursing gunshot wounds and she seriously lost respect in the eyes of her soldiers. As she demanded someone be held responsible the lights were switched back on and in place of the girls stood her son, Eric.

He stood there with his arms crossed and his legs wide apart as if he had recently landed from a distant planet.

"Mother, I think you've done enough damage for one day. Captain, please escort my mother to her rooms and make sure she is kept there until I have time to decide on what to do with her." He pointed his finger at his mother and then gestured she should leave him.

"You bumble headed young fool. I've done all this for you. You've no idea what is possible if you have a bit of guts to do the unthinkable. Kingdoms lie before you. Dominions without end. Who knows but we could unite the countries of Africa and rule as Shaka did in days gone by."Atalia hissed.

"Shaka? Do you think I want to be like Shaka? He murdered two million of his own people. He even killed his own concubines when they fell pregnant so he wouldn't have to be fearful of his own children taking over from him when he grew old. Why would I want a life so debauched?"

Shaking his head emphatically he said.

"No Mother, I'm not a Shaka or even a Dingaan, rather I hope to be Eric the benevolent or the kind. I want history to remember me with respect and awe at what could be achieved through peaceful methods. Mother you need to leave now before I say something terrible to you. Go, go."

The corridors of the palace filled with half-dressed sleepy landed gentry. They watched as Atalia was marched to her rooms under guard. No one whispered a word as she did the walk of shame with her head held high but visibly shaking all over. The guard had to open her door because her hands were unable to grasp the door handle.

Her ladies-in-waiting gathered around her to help her sit down and they rubbed her shoulders in an effort to calm her down. Another lady poured some camomile tea and another put a footstool under the Queen's feet. The door closed on the gaping audience and Atalia felt hot tears coursing down her cheeks.

By dawn she had concocted a plan of attack. She sifted through her box of poisons and frantically chose the three most vicious potions.

Eric came to see her after breakfast was finished. Atalia ate in her rooms because she found her door barred when she tried to leave. A prisoner in her own home. A gilded cage for an exotic flightless bird. Eric sat down in the chair opposite his mother and leaned forward slightly so he could pat her hand gently.

"Mother, I'm sorry it has come to this. I hoped you could learn to appreciate my leadership style, but sadly you are incapable of it. I know you want to poison me. Yes, Mother, don't deny it. I know how you schemed and manipulated my brothers and sisters to get me to this position."

Sighing sadly. He looked keenly at his mother.

"I wish I could change what you have done, but I'm stuck with the consequences of your actions. I cry to think you killed a gentle man like my Father because he didn't die when it was convenient to you. He knew what you were planning and still loved you enough to hope you wouldn't carry through your intentions. Yes, he did know everything.

"And no, he didn't tell me any of this. He left a letter with the Sangoma, but even without the letter, I would've known and it has broken my heart."

Eric sipped a glass of orange juice and let the conversation sink in for his mother. "I'll endeavour to undo some of your evil plans Mother, but there are some things too late to fix. I've demanded Namaqua and Per leave. Their friendship was based on fickle things and I don't need friends in my life who I can't trust. We'll have the ball next week as planned and then you'll be taken to the mountains and set up in a home where I hope you'll contemplate your choices, but I doubt it'll bring you much peace. I can't sink to your level and kill you.

"I have instructed your ladies-in-waiting to remove all your poisons and potions and not to purchase any more for your use. Your reign of terror will end here and now. Understood?"

Atalia flew out of her chair with nails like talons as she tried to scratch Eric's eyes out. He easily fended her off and the guards had her restrained. A doctor came forward and administered an injection to calm her down. She slumped forward and Eric called forward her courtiers to catch her before she injured herself. Her ladies carried her to bed and then systematically searched her room for the noxious potions, her signature means of revenge.

Eric shook each of their hands after they were finished and some of the ladies were immediately dismissed with a hefty financial reward, while those who were to the King's taste were given instructions on how to treat his mother.

Lady Sofia was sent to the new home to make it ready for the Queen. She was given carte blanche to stock it with everything worthy of a queen. Lady Teresia was asked to pack the clothing and personal jewellery not needed immediately and could be sent ahead. Eric spent the morning vetting the guards in the palace and by dinner time he was absolutely exhausted. The process of looking into people's darkest character flaws had sapped his strength and he needed some respite.

Nkomo and Nyama had taken off with their daughter and Per during the day and dinner was a much more subdued event. Chef outdid himself with the food and Eric proclaimed he had never before had such a delightful meal.

The Chief engineer and some of his staff came forward and set up plinths on the dance floor. Each plinth had a beautifully crafted engineering marvel. Some were made of base metals, but there were those shimmering in the light of the chandeliers with rich colours of different hues. Each piece was admired and the engineer who had made it was given a reward of gold coins hastily requisitioned from the treasury.

The final piece was kept under a cover and when Eric reached it the velvet cloth was removed to reveal two crowns made of gold and diamonds so fine they almost floated on their cushion.

"For your official coronation, my Lord."

"But there are two crowns, Frederick. Do you know something I am not aware of? Is one of them for my Mother perhaps?"

"No, my liege, the smaller crown is for your future Queen, one who is worthy to wear this creation. Someone with a heart of gold and a mind of great intelligence to match your own."

Eric laughed a great guffaw of a laugh and clasped Frederick the Chief engineer's hand in pleasure. "I know exactly the lady who would be perfect for this role, but we'll need to convince her it's a good idea to take on someone like me."

Frederick laughed along with his king. Eric went off to have an early night. It was like he had been awake for days and had achieved so much causing his body to ache. The creation of the crowns was the light relief Eric needed before relaxing after the stress of the past two days.

He fell asleep as soon as his head touched the pillow and didn't wake up even when his mother caused a commotion in her rooms. She ripped furnishings and clothes. She screamed and yelled obscenities demanding her dismissed ladies-in-waiting be recalled. She threw open drawers in search of her potions saying she had no option but to kill herself now she was stripped of her authority. Vases were smashed and mirrors shattered in the frenzy.

She wore herself out finally and then sat with a large glass of brandy muttering to herself in the ruined rooms. She wandered around kicking out at anything getting in her way and her ladies in waiting made sure the palace cats and dog were safe and well out of Atalia's reach.

CHAPTER TWENTY TWO

Eric was briefed at breakfast about his mother's tantrum and sent her a few servants to help clean up the mess. The rest of the day was spent with the party planners and designers. He had no idea there was so much involved in planning a ball. There were flowers to approve, meals to plan, decorations and entertainment, seating plans and accommodations.

The replies to the invites piled up and Eric had to send for the carpenters to erect temporary glamping tents for people to use while there. Great wooden floors raised the tents off the ground and covered walkways were constructed. The plains in front of the palace resembled a gathering of all the tribes of Africa in one place.

Some of those who had declined the invite earlier, now changed their minds and phoned to insist it had been a mistake or misunderstanding and they would never miss this occasion for anything. Historical was a word bandied about. Ragnar hustled between king and courtiers, guests and servants from dawn to dusk doing Eric's bidding.

Two days later Eric was fed up with the minutiae and dramas connected with the ball. He phoned his brother Cedric and his partner and begged them to please come and take over. Cedric was more than happy to heal the rift in the family and after a manic day of shopping in Paris, Cedric and Francis boarded a specially hired jet and flew across Europe and Africa to arrive by the next morning. Francis took over the preparations with barely a moment to recover from jet lag while Cedric sat with his brother and caught up on the family dramas.

They phoned their brother Claude in Switzerland and convinced him to come home. A special room was prepared free of allergens and equipped with the best medical care for his breathing difficulties. They were surprised to hear he had a fiancé who would accompany him, with her mother as chaperone.

The sisters and their husbands and children of various ages were accommodated in one of the glamping camps with their own playground and hastily erected spa pool and swimming hole.

Each tent was equipped with solar powered air conditioners, large TVs and gaming consoles. The royal treasury groaned at the seams as the cost of this grand event took its toll. Accountants joined in the throng surrounding the King and he found himself beleaguered in his own palace.

Eric had not thought of his mother for days and existed from moment to moment. He might not like his mother, but she did have skills in organization and these were sorely missed.

Cedric started to fade in the heat and demanded a day off to have a massage and pamper day with Francis. Eric promised them both a spa week at a Swiss resort as soon as the circus of ceremonies was over.

The day arrived for the ball and Eric felt the world had come to a stop. No more organising to do, no more people to appease or cajole.

He spent the morning at the pool while Claude lazed around on an inflatable lounger. Claude and Cedric both admitted to having the gift of discernment and using it for their own means. It felt good to bond with his brothers.

After lunch, he went to visit his sister's camps and became acquainted with their children and husbands. The women were primped and preened and the husbands were happy to sit in the shade and have a quiet moment before they too were expected to put on their glad rags.

Claude was happy to tag along and introduced his future wife to his family. She was like a miniature doll with the smallest hands anyone could ever remember seeing.

The nieces and nephews immediately took a liking to her and she was surrounded by giggling teenagers and curious children. Claude took her home before she became too exhausted. He looked forward to showing her off at the ball and proudly ushered her into a carriage for the ride back.

By five o'clock Eric was back in his rooms having a light meal and a massage of his own. He was pummelled and oiled with sweet smelling oils until he felt all relaxed and lethargic. A servant brought in his freshly ironed clothes and he dressed slowly so as not to become over heated.

The ball started with a family dinner held in the great hall with even the children being invited to attend. After the informal meal, a marching band lead the way for the royal procession, starting at the gates and winding its way through the gardens before finally arriving at the ball room.

Cedric and Francis had not allowed Eric to view the finished room and were quietly excited to see the reactions.

Atalia was led out to take her place alongside her son and gently laid her hand on his arm as the band started their repertoire. Cedric and Francis took their place behind them and so it went until all the royals had assembled.

At a signal from the drum major Eric and Atalia started walking. They waved to all their guests and stopped to shake the hands of some of them. Little children ran forward with bouquets of flowers to present and Eric made sure to bow down so he could look them eye to eye as he thanked them for the gift.

A courtier was given the job of taking the offerings when they became too much to handle. Atalia barely acknowledged the children and ignored many of the clamouring crowd.

At the door of the ballroom Eric stopped to admire the scene. Great chandeliers hung from the ceiling as was to be expected, but it was the plethora of crystal orbs hanging from the roof catching the light and refracting it into a rainbow of magic. The walls were covered in hanging gardens of white and gold flowers perfuming the air with gentle scents.

Even Claude, with his asthma, was able to admire them and not have an adverse reaction. He had his inhaler at hand, but it stayed in his pocket the whole night through. The band members were also clothed in white and gold and played a gentle tune to soothe the wildest heart.

Eric placed his mother on a throne and instructed the guard to make sure she did not leave, but to do it discreetly. The guard nodded in agreement. But finally, Eric could look around and search for the one face he had waited to see. He had almost given up when a minor disturbance was seen at the door and there through the crowd came Alpheus and his three wives, then Ndlovu and Izzie.

They stopped and bowed to the King and then stepped aside so Phoebe could be revealed. She shimmered with an inner light as she glided across the floor. Even the band stopped playing in awe of her beauty. A filigree of silver and gold encased her body and underneath the metal was a soft material of white silk. The metal was connected to the dress with a myriad of tiny pearls.

Phoebe did not wear any jewellery and her honey coloured skin shone like the sun. Eric reached for her hand and signalled to the band to play the opening tune. Eric whirled around his princess and then beckoned to Cedric and Francis and Claude and Mary to join them.

The three couples wove their way around the floor and invited their sisters to join them. Within minutes, the floor was a cornucopia of colours as the peacock colours of the women and the muted tones of the men meshed together.

Eric did not want to relinquish Phoebe to any of the other eager young men but protocol demanded he dance with at least a few of the other women. Every time he turned around he saw Phoebe being escorted through the dance steps by another grinning male. Surprised they had been the recipient of her company, they bumbled through stilted conversations and blushed wildly as she answered them with grace and kindness.

Alpheus took the floor with his daughter for the final dance before supper was served. Nyoni, Thandi and Sarah paid their respects to Atalia and they noticed a few others approaching the throne at times during the night. But the Queens scowl did not lift.

After supper, the obligatory 'thank you' speeches were given. Cedric acted as master of ceremonies and people laughed at his quick wit and terrible jokes. The citizens of the country were pleased to see a united royal family and laughed louder than was necessary for the pleasure of it all.

Eric finally stood up to give his speech and for a moment was lost for words. "Cedric and Francis, what can I say? You've created a wonderland this country has not seen in the last thousand years at least. Your hard work has borne the most amazing fruit, thank you from the bottom of my heart and the depths of the royal treasury."

He looked around to find where his family were standing.

"To my family, thank you for joining me for this night of celebration. Family united in love and hard work have reminded me of what life is truly about.

"And to my sweet Phoebe, you won my heart a few months ago but tonight you have won my admiration for your poise and grace. Thank you for being part of my life."

Turning slightly, he looked down at his mother and his eyes turned cold as he contemplated her.

"To my mother, Atalia, I can't tell you what is in my mind but know I admire your dedication to your cause and your focused mind in all you do. Thank you for showing me where I should go and what I should do."

Spreading his arms wide he encompassed the crowd.

"To all my honoured guests. Your company has been a joy to me. Your efforts to get here have lifted my spirits. And now to all the people behind the scenes, I can't thank you enough. When we're all in our beds you will be busy cleaning. When we're snoring, you'll be washing the dishes and scrubbing the floors. Never forget without you this would never have been possible. The decorations are spectacular. The food superb, the music divine and the ambience heavenly. I'm in awe of your skills and your talents.

"And finally, to all the workmen who built the accommodations. They're fabulous. If I didn't already have a sumptuous bed to sleep in I would be more than happy to stay in your tents. How about a round of applause for all their hard work folks?"

The ball room erupted in a cacophony of clapping and cheering. Cedric gave a signal to the unseen actors behind the scenes and the ball room was filled with stilt walkers and ribbon weavers along with tumbling gymnasts and twirling dancers.

From the ceiling, silken ropes descended and brightly coloured artistes tumbled down in a controlled fall. A group of Air Whisperers walked across the ceiling, trailing coloured feather tails trimmed with crystals. The flame people metamorphosed into wisps of flame and the heat from their fires caused paper lanterns to swirl through the air.

The chandeliers were switched off and the ball room became a wonderland of fantasy. An origami specialist from Japan created ten thousand paper cranes flitting down above head height on gossamer threads. Oohs and aahs were heard as the older people admired the skills and the younger guests wondered at the spectacle. When the guests had thought the show could not get better, it did. The stilt walkers twirled in feats of gymnastic prowess. The paper origami cranes were replaced with leaping paper frogs making people jump in surprise and fun. The air whisperers and fire people adapted their show to fit around the other performers. Showers of rose petals floated on the air currents created by fire people with flames dancing around their heads.

The show finished with a flourish and then the performers left to enjoy their own celebrations out in the gardens. Tired but pleased with their evenings actions. Many of them patting each other on their backs and giving high fives in celebration.

The band started playing again at the signal of the King and many of the older guests made ready to leave. The younger people were eager for more dancing. Eric saw Rachel being taught the basics of the jive by two young men who looked like twins but Phoebe was nowhere to be seen.

Ragnar whispered to him she had left after the band had restarted and could not have gone far. He finally found her sitting on a bench in the garden staring up at the stars. Without him saying a word she sensed he was there and she patted the bench next to her.

He put his arm around her and they leaned together in companionship. The music played softly in the background till dawn and it was only as the sky turned pink, Eric stood up. "We should go. I could do with some breakfast."

Hand in hand they ambled down the quiet passageways.

They found the buffet table now cleared and laid with a selection of cold dishes for breakfast. They ate in silence and then Ragnar and Cedric came in to join them. Ragnar was already dressed in his usual buttoned up shirt and smart slacks and Cedric in an exotic silken wrap.

They all chatted about the ball and the highlights. Phoebe said she needed to get back to her family and have a sleep for a few hours. Eric kissed her lightly on the nose and forehead. Phoebe waved goodbye to the others as she strode out of the dining room.

Cedric went back to bed to see if Francis was awake and interested in a day of inactivity around the pool. Ragnar and Eric had things to discuss and went off to his office to talk in private.

CHAPTER TWENTY THREE

"I'd like to marry Phoebe, Ragnar but I don't think the coffers of the royal house can withstand another onslaught like the ball. Maybe a quiet ceremony including her family and ours. Do you have any suggestions? I know I'm asking a lot of you when we've barely finished one celebration and I'm expecting another one. But we thought maybe in a few months?"

The treasury books were opened and the two men bent their heads over the books for the rest of the morning. They sat with a glass of juice each when a frantic guard dashed into the room.

"The Queen has escaped, Sir. Her guards were found drugged about ten minutes ago and it appears she might've left during the night, perhaps during the festivities. Do you want me to send out the troops?"

"I think we can use your future mother-in-law, Eric. She can fly above the area and see where your mother might've gone and how many people she has with her."

"Great idea, Ragnar. Guard, can you send word to the Air Whisperers. I urgently need to speak to Nyoni."

Eric looked down at his wrinkled suit from the night before and asked Ragnar to mind the fort, he went off to have a quick shower and dress in fresh clothes before dealing with this latest drama. His hair still dripping wet and while still putting on his shoes he heard the Air Whisperers coming into his rooms. Ragnar seated them all in the lounge and updated them on what they knew.

"Why don't you let your mother go Eric? Maybe this is for the best?" Alpheus advised.

"I know my mother is capable of causing trouble and I would rather avoid it at this moment. When things were going perfectly, she has seen our unity as a weakness and is no doubt planning on how to capitalize on what she sees as an opportunity. Nyoni, if you could fly over the area and find out where they are and with whom, we can then assess the situation better."

He opened his windows and Nyoni flew out above their heads. Izzie and Ndlovu offered to send out a sub audio message to all the animals in the country to keep a look out. They did this by standing at the window and issuing a deep rumble into the ether.

Nyoni came back about an hour later to say Atalia had met up with Nyama and Nkomo over the border of Namibia. She was unable to get close enough to hear what they were saying but there was a large contingent of soldiers with them. They had armed themselves with weapons lethal and destructive.

It would take quite some time for them to return to Zululand and she was sure the Queen must have flown to Namibia because there was no land transport able to have reached there in less than a day. The soldiers were in troop carriers but even they would need two days to travel back to the borders of Zululand.

"How did you find them so quickly? Surely Namibia is too far for even you to have flown there and back in an hour?"

Nyoni laughed. "Of course, but I spoke to the eagles and hawks of the air and they in turn spoke to the seagulls and owls. When I knew where they were I caught a thermal and was there so fast even I was stunned at the speed. I only stayed a few minutes before catching a returning thermal. I was so high up it would have been impossible for them to see me. I would've been a flash of something small in the air for only a moment."

"Well, at least it gives us time to gather our troops and make plans. Ragnar can you ask the captains to assemble their men and I'll address them at sundown."

A large map was unrolled and laid on the floor so all could see what they were up against. Possible routes were surveyed and Ndlovu and Izzie went out to see what animals were able to help.

By the end of the day reports were received from the elephants of the Namib, the fowls of the air and even the various royal siblings had rallied to the cause. The atmosphere was totally different to the previous night. The dress was more practical, the attitudes more defined and the harmony made the air hum with purpose.

CHAPTER TWENTY FOUR

Phoebe had been left to sleep by her family and by the time she woke up the world had changed. She had gone to bed dreaming of a beautiful peaceful wedding and woke up to a war. She sat stunned in Eric's office when the phone rang and she automatically picked it up.

"Hi, this is Eric's phone, can I help you? He is unable to come to the phone right now."

"Grease monkey? How dare you answer the King's phone? Put Eric on the line immediately." Namaqua could be heard yelling by everyone in the room.

He lifted his eyebrows as he answered the phone. "Yes, Namaqua. What can I help you with? We're a bit busy at the moment. My Mom has gone missing and we're trying to find out what has happened to her." He had no qualms about lying to Namaqua. She no longer fitted into the category of trusted friend. He had seen into her heart and did not trust her in the least.

"Oh, Eric my sweetie. My soul was so hurt I missed your ball. I know you must've been devastated I was not there. But you know how it goes, Daddy holds the purse strings and I have to go with what he wants. He phoned me in Paris and insisted I come home and not to go to your celebration and I could not refuse.

"Did you say your Mom is missing? Really? How awful. She is one of the sweetest ladies I know. Do you want me to come and stand by your side? I will defy Daddy if you want me there. You need strong people around you now and I can be a great strength. You can get rid of the grease monkey and I can be your companion, now and always." She breathed down the line.

"No, Namaqua. It would not suit me at the moment. I have all my siblings with me and I think you would be a distraction," Ragnar signalled to Eric to read a note he had written. "But maybe it would be good if you could come when you're able. Yes, it would be great. Thank you for being such a fantastic caring friend. Let me know what flight you're taking and I'll send a driver to pick you up."

Eric frowned at Ragnar as he repeated this and Phoebe was totally confused at this sudden change of tactic.

"Leverage, Eric. Namaqua will be our way of controlling the situation. She'll think you trust her and we can use her to feed disinformation to her father and your mother. We'll have to play along and maybe Phoebe will need to stay away from you, because quite frankly, when the two of you are in the same room there is no doubting you have eyes for her only, and we want Namaqua to think she still has you all tied up with lust or whatever."

Eric's sisters and their children left to return to their homes so they did not get in the way of all this soldiering. Claude returned to Switzerland as his asthma reacted to the excitement but he promised to send what support he could. Cedric and Francis likewise did not think they would be very useful and were happy to return home with instructions to plan a small wedding for later in the year.

In fact, Claude thought they might have a double wedding if everyone was amenable.

Ndlovu and two of the brothers in law were sent west to start ambushes along the most likely routes of travel. Alpheus and the three pachyderm soldiers were to train the troops in different forms of fighting, while the captains of the king's guard set up target practice.

The engineers showed Eric and Ragnar the intricacies of their creations but as they had been commissioned by the Queen they were not confident anything they had would be a surprise. Phoebe sat with the Chief engineer and they added surprises to the armaments. Things the Queen would not be expecting.

Phoebe worked alongside the engineers as they worked through the night to prepare what they could. When Namaqua arrived, Phoebe had her nose to a literal grindstone in the workshops. Per had come with her but he was happy to spend his time in the gym or at the pool totally disinterested in the preparations for war. They were not shown the preparations. Rather, Eric acted the concerned son worried about the safety of his beloved mother.

He showed Namaqua pictures of the beautiful home he had prepared for his mother and bemoaned the fact some evil force might be preventing her from enjoying her retirement.

At no stage did anyone mention the Queen might have left of her own free will. They were all instructed to play along with the story of the Queen being abducted. As far as Namaqua was concerned there were no preparations for battle at all.

Dinner was served as normal in the evening without a sign of stress from the king, only concern. Ragnar whispered in his ear at times but none of the courtiers were aware things were not as usual. Ragnar organised a display by the Japanese origami artist to show Namaqua a smidgen of what she had missed at the ball.

The fire sprites showed off their skills and the company were amused at how Namaqua enjoyed her special display. She did complain the culture in Africa did not hold a candle to things she enjoyed in Europe. Eric shrugged and smiled at his unwelcome guest.

She snuggled up to him and chatted about her amazing life in Europe and how she wanted her future husband to be supportive of her international lifestyle. As she said this she smiled coyly at Eric and leaned forward to kiss him full on the mouth. Giggling she took herself off to bed.

Looking over her shoulder she said, "We can continue this conversation in my boudoir if you like Eric sweetie."

"Too busy tonight sweetie. Maybe some other time." Eric called as he removed himself to his bedroom.

The following morning Eric was informed the Queen and her forces had crossed the border and were within a day of the palace. Thandi managed to infiltrate their meeting and overheard their plans. E'Showe and his forest sprites massed alongside the Queen and she now had several thousand troops at her command.

Nkomo supplied food for them all as his contribution to the war effort and of course they were being fed information from Namaqua via internet and phone. The Queen was overjoyed they would find the Zulus unprepared for war and she could affect a bloodless coup.

Under cover of darkness Phoebe and the engineers had moved their weaponry into strategic spots along the mountain passes. If the Queen had scouts in advance of the war party, they were not evident and Eric hoped his mother was so sure of victory, she was complacent and not bothered with them.

At breakfast Namaqua and Per sat on either side of Eric and offered him any help in finding his mother. Had he received a kidnapping demand, some sort of ransom? Maybe they could help deliver it.

As if on cue a letter was handed to Eric with exactly such a demand. He read it out to the gathered people and shook his head, as if in sadness at the perfidy of mankind. "What has my Mother ever done to deserve this great treachery?" He bemoaned.

He went off to supposedly find a way to pay the ransom and Namaqua and Per went off to report to the Queen their plan worked perfectly. By lunchtime there was no more hiding what was really happening and Eric instructed the guards to remove the cell phones and internet devices from the two guests and to make sure they were kept comfortable but confined until further notice.

They were hoping Namaqua and Per would be oblivious to the change of circumstances for a few more hours, but they were not so lucky. As Eric and Ragnar left the palace they could hear the screaming of Namaqua as she demanded to know what was happening. The element of surprise was essential to success.

Nyoni reported the Queen was now within two hours of the palace and entered the ambush site totally oblivious to the gathered troops surrounding their position. She stopped for lunch and for a final briefing. When Eric and Ragnar wandered into their campsite, as if by mistake, the shock of the Queen and her minions was palpable.

"Mother. Welcome home. Nyama, Nkomo, I see you have returned. E'Showe, I did not know you were joining this little party, you should've let me know and I would've sent a welcome committee." He smiled at them as if pleased to see some honoured guests come to visit in peace.

The Queen did not answer and the others mumbled a greeting of sorts. Atalia beckoned over a few men and announced in a loud voice. "Arrest this man. He's no longer king. From now on he'll live in exile and I'll be the ruler of this land."

As the men moved forward a single shot rang out and hit the ground in front of them. "Ah, Mother, did you think I would be foolish enough to come alone." At his signal, a wall of soldiers appeared at the top of the kloof.

"Ah son, did you think I was stupid enough to believe the spying of an addled headed young woman."

157

Arrows rained down on the men on the kloof and they fought for their lives. Eric and Ragnar beat a hasty retreat back the way they had come.

Puffing slightly, they laughed and agreed it was perhaps for the better things had turned out this way. Now they would know for sure who their enemies really were. The battles raged all day and as night fell it was if the world took a deep breath and paused for a moment before the night attacks by guerrillas started. Both sides sustained losses and injuries.

By morning the Queen had taken the high ground of the kloof, unfortunately the way forward was blocked as was the retreat. The Queen and her forces were boxed in and Eric called a break in the fighting so they could negotiate a truce so some of the wounded could be attended to.

Medics descended on the battle fields and a triage hospital was set up further down the valley. Doctors and surgeons worked on the result of a senseless battle.

At lunch time, the truce was over and the fighting started again. Great sky ships fought in the air above their heads, trundling machines hauled weapons of horror onto the battlefield. The heights were bombarded with all Phoebe and the engineers had concocted. An outside observer might think the flashes and different coloured smoke were entertaining but for those in the thick of the fighting it wasn't.

At one stage Ragnar found himself fighting man to man with a strange creature resembling a forest vine and he gave a nervous little laugh as he thought it would be amusing to tell his grandchildren the story of his bravery against a piece of flora if he could survive the battle. He had now been fighting for almost a whole day and he looked around to see if he could see Eric.

Ragnar saw his friend, standing shoulder to shoulder with Alpheus, fighting off a handful of large angry men with swords. Alpheus only had his fighting stick with him and made inroads against the larger force. As Ragnar watched Alpheus smacked one man on the head and dropped him like a stone.

Alpheus's wives systematically attacked the men on the periphery of the fighting, taking them into the sky and dropping them with deadly accuracy on their fellow soldiers. This could not continue on for much longer as the numbers of the enemy dwindled by the minute. Piles of injured and exhausted men littered the fields as far as the eye could see.

Xele, Isifunda and Tembe had great sport changing from human to pachyderm to bamboozle the offenders. Finally, Eric was able to stop for a breather and he realised his legs shook with adrenaline.

Alpheus and Ragnar each took an arm and helped Eric to a log. Thandi appeared with a bottle of iced water for the thirsty men. Nyoni flew down with a handful of nuts for each of the men and then flew off to see where else she could be of assistance.

There were only small pockets of resistance and even they surrendered in defeat. A deep rumble could be heard from the elephant people as they celebrated the end of fighting. Eric was sickened by the carnage around him. He walked through the fields stopping to give help where he could and looked to see if he could find his mother. He saw her sitting on a rock with tears rolling down her cheeks in anger, muttering to herself about next time things would be different.

"Eric, you're a disappointment to me. If you had listened to reason, all these fine men and women wouldn't have had to fight and be killed or injured. It is all your fault. Stupid boy, you're too much like your father."

Eric stood looking down at her and felt Phoebe softly land next to him. She took his hand in a gentle grip. She ran her fingers over his fingertips and smiling sweetly she leaned down and whispered to Atalia. "Don't speak to your son in such a disrespectful manner. He's a fine man and a great leader. He cares for his people and history will remember him as a force for good."

Atalia looked at Phoebe as if she were slightly mad and to be pitied. She gathered her wits about her to give a withering reply when Phoebe took Eric by both his hands and the two of them rose up in the air leaving Atalia half way through her retort.

They glided to the top of the kloof so Eric could survey his troops. Nyama and Nkomo still sat in their carriage as they had done through the battle. Nkomo called to non-existent servants to bring them food before they died of starvation.

"This is shameful. I have low blood sugar and need to eat at least ten times a day. Food, where is something for me to eat Nkomo?"

Nkomo in his own defence was stuck in a chair so tightly it would have taken a crane to lever him out. He lifted his hands in defeat and looked around for inspiration.

Finally, Nyama levered her great bulk out of her seat and waddled around the camp site until she found a cache of biscuits. She took them back to her husband. They looked totally unimpressed by what had taken place and urged their bullocks to pull their wagon back the way they had come.

They found some straggling survivors along the way and with the promise of great wealth the servants were coerced back to serving them. They showed no remorse or even concern for their daughter, now held captive in the palace at Ulundi, and were soon sleeping on soft mattresses as the wagon wound its way back home.

E'Showe limped off with a few of his wood sprites in attendance and Eric commanded his soldiers not to bother chasing them but rather for them to care for their compatriots and then get themselves home to their families. The women of the villages began to emerge from the fields like magic and tended to cuts and bruises and the few dead.

The ululation from these women carried through the air as they sung their songs of sadness and grief and touched the hearts of all who heard them. The elephant people were happy to change into their pachyderm personas and be used to carry the injured to hospitals and homes.

Eric and Phoebe were everywhere. Giving food and drink to the soldiers, offering money to help with funerals, a kind word given and hugs of comfort. Nyoni and Thandi used their powers to ease pain and suffering and, as the sun sank below the horizon, the family all returned to the palace.

Ragnar organised a cold buffet for them all and had hot baths with healing salts run in the rooms. Too tired to think, they grabbed a muffin or a guava and stumbled to any room they could find. The elephant people moved into the glamping camp and were fast asleep as the stars flickered to life in the heavens.

Thandi gave the family all an herbal tea to help with any anxiety or stress they might be feeling keeping them from sleep but no one needed it as they sank into soft mattresses. Only Ragnar and Eric were left to walk the halls and make sure all was safe. They stopped at the rooms where Namaqua and Per were to tell them the outcome of the battle.

Namaqua tried her best to pretend she wasn't spying but Eric had none of her lies. He advised them they could go home tomorrow and they were to be banned from his kingdom for the foreseeable future.

"Don't think I'm a soft fool. I'm releasing you because your evil machinations tire me out and I have happier things to concentrate on. Ragnar will make sure you're escorted to the airport and given passage to where ever you want, within reason. Be sure to be up and packed for travel by breakfast time."

Namaqua stood with her mouth open in shock. "Eric sweetie, surely you don't mean it. We are your best friends in the whole world. Don't be like this. This is partly your own fault you know, if you hadn't tried to replace us with a grease monkey and this rag bag of a man, we would've never sided with Mumsy and Daddy. We were a teensy bit jealous. Weren't we, Persie?"

Ragnar and Eric looked at each other and laughed. "Sorry Namaqua and Per, your goose is well and truly cooked. Take this exile with good grace and you can keep some of your dignity. I'm going to marry my grease monkey one day soon and Ragnar is not only my friend, he is my brother in every way except blood. I trust them with my life. You I trust with nothing. Hambane Gahle, go well and do not darken this land again."

The two men turned and walked away as Namaqua screamed obscenities at their backs. The guard smiled at his king and locked the doors to the rooms with a big smile on his face.

The morning dawned on a perfect day of blue skies and warm breezes. Eric was dressed in all the pomp and ceremony of his rank and Phoebe resurrected her ball dress to wear as she took her place beside him. The first order of business was to bid farewell to their unwelcome guests and then to visit the families of the soldiers from the battle to thank them and their families for all they had sacrificed. Eric held tight to Phoebe's hand as they stood shoulder to shoulder to face the day.

Alpheus, Thandi, Nyoni and Sarah stood behind them every step of the way. They were so proud of Phoebe and how much she had matured over the past two years. The first few days of running from the troops of the evil Queen. Then the months with the elephant people now Phoebe had eventually come into her own with the engineers. The abduction and her actions to protect her sisters. Now this gem of a woman who stood with such dignity in the homes and sickrooms of the poor people of the land was a sight to behold.

She did not flinch as a child with sticky fingers touched the pearls on her dress or a man, badly mutilated, wanted to give her a hug. By the end of the day her dress was much the worse for wear and Eric suggested they raid the wardrobes of the royal household to find her something else.

"If we have to do these visits for a few more days, my dear, you'll need other outfits." Eric smiled at Phoebe as he said this.

Tembe stepped forward. "Phoebe, I made all those dresses for your family for the ball, maybe we can adapt a few of them. They can be hosed down at the end of the day too and they'll be good as new."

The next few days went by in a whirlwind of activity. It was quite a surprise to wake up one morning and have nothing to do. No more sick room visits, no more funerals to attend, no families to comfort or console. They had all woken up early each day and fallen into bed at night, exhausted and aching with tiredness.

Alpheus and his family returned to their home to rebuild what was destroyed. The elephant people had packed up and marched off into the sunset the night before and the palace was empty. There were only six people at breakfast instead of the usual dozen or so. Eric sat and looked over at Phoebe.

Rachel and Tembe stayed on as her chaperones and attendants. Sipho worked alongside Ragnar to learn how to run a royal household.

"Ragnar what have you got for us today? Are there court cases to hear? Disputes about land or cattle? What is my agenda, my friend?"

Ragnar looked up with a twinkle in his eye. "Well yes, I do have an urgent assignment and it requires your attendance my liege. A new theme park is being opened and they have asked for your blessing. I suggested the six of us go there and test some of the rides for the day. It's not open to the public yet, so we'll have free rein. I call dibs on the red bumper car. I've always loved red and I think I can beat the rest of you with one hand tied behind my back."

"You are an overconfident. You have no hope. I have seen you drive and I know you are as slow as a snail." laughed Eric.

The six of them scrambled off to find clothes appropriate for a day of fun in the sun. Ragnar had taken Sipho under his wing and looked on him as a younger brother to be moulded but not today. Today was all about fun and to let the best person win.

Eric took Phoebe by the hand and the two of them tried out the tunnel of love while the other friends all rolled their eyes and made kissing sounds with their mouths as they dashed off to find more exciting pursuits. They had not a care in the world and for a while could pretend they were normal. Eric and Phoebe emerged flushed and rosy cheeked at the end of their ride while the others could be heard screaming at the top of their lungs as the roller coaster reached its zenith. The bumper car ride had them all vying for position. Ragnar did indeed get his red car to ride, but was no match for Tembe as she bumped everyone with impunity, giving fist bumps at each collision. Sipho was a close second and the two friends stood triumphant at the end of the day. Claiming victory over the others at their ability to handle the scariest rides and number of prizes won. Phoebe held a fluffy white monkey Eric had won at the shooting range and Rachel happily cuddled a bright green frog she had won herself at whack-a-mole. It was a day filled with fun and was the perfect antidote to their previous few weeks of drama.

Atalia looked out the window of her mountain top prison. Whatever she requested was granted and she devised a way of bribing the delivery man to sneak in some illicit drugs and potions, if her son knew about would cause him grave concern. She did not expect a visit from her son any time soon. Her spies had revealed to her he was more than busy with his duties with the simpering girl, Phoebe, ever at his side. Her attendants were instructed to watch her, but she was working on them slowly. Finding out their secrets and desires so when she wanted to escape she knew of them would most likely be her best bet.

She heard there was a wedding being planned and had no desire to be left out of the celebrations. Surely Eric would bring her to his nuptials. When he was distracted she would pounce and regain her power. Captain Raz was now free of his prison at the Ndlovu kingdom and had made his way to her abode.

A note here, a bribe there was all it took for him to be hired as the gardener for the fortress. He was not a very convincing gardener, but Atalia did not mind a few weeds and Raz was happy to be planning the downfall of the king once again.

CHAPTER TWENTY FIVE

"Dad, Mom I know you always said I would know when I met the man of my dreams. My life's companion. Well I think it is Eric. No, let me rephrase, I am sure it is Eric."

"You're so young, too young to get married. You have recently turned nineteen, for goodness sake. Your life is barely starting." Nyoni spoke what was in the minds of the other adults present at this family dinner. The village had been rebuilt but they were all tired from all the hard work required and not in the mood for teenage dramas.

Alpheus stepped forward and looked deeply into Phoebe's eyes. "Is this really what you want? As a queen you will be expected to give up your dreams of being an engineer. Of travelling the world helping others. Of building machines to amaze people far and wide."

"Yes Dad. I can still do a lot of those things and I'll continue to study and learn from the best."

"But as the wife of a king, your life will be forfeit to the needs of the nation. Can you handle it all?" Urged Thandi.

"Oh, Thandi of course my life will change, but life doesn't stay the same no matter the path I take. And this is a path I have chosen. And I love him more than I ever imagined."

"Well then I think it is time we celebrated. Who wants to carry me to the top of the big Tamboti tree? Nyoni? Sarah? or what about you my daughter, you want to take on new burdens. Maybe you can carry me?"

Laughing and joking the women took turns in ferrying the little children and boys to the top of the trees. Alpheus regaled them with tales of when he was a child.

"My Auntie Mary would often take me on her back to the top of trees and I would tell her to go home so I could speak to nature. One day she left me sitting on a forest vine thinking I would cry when she left. But I was happily chatting away to the Stinkwood tree like we were best of mates. She said it was the funniest thing she had ever seen."

"Oh, but I have something better than Alpheus's story." Assured Nyoni. "When I was a little girl my cousin, Atalia the Zulu Queen begged me to help her learn to fly. We climbed a cliff and using an old bed sheet, we strapped it to her back. She looked like a crazy bat person with it on her arms and legs. Well of course she fell and injured herself quite badly and had to go to hospital for ages. And me, well my Mom took me to a tall tree and left me there all night to think about what I had done. She told me later she was an arms-length away at all times, but it was super scary all the same."

Phoebe leaned back against her father's legs and smiled at all the stories until she drifted off to sleep right in the middle   of   a   long,   long   tale.

CHAPTER TWENTY SIX

The year had flown by and Eric would be twenty-two. Phoebe was through her first year of university with flying colours and decided a wedding would be perfect during her long summer holidays. She missed Eric when they were apart and knew he felt the same. He was busy fixing what his mother had destroyed. People now trusted in their royal family once again.

Cedric and Claude were often guests at the palace and Claude married in a simple ceremony in Switzerland to his sweetheart, Mary. They had decided to have a quiet ceremony with just a few close friends and family. Cedric was hired to renovate the royal quarters, ready for when Phoebe moved in. Many calls, many shopping trips, and even more swatches and mood boards had filled up each spare moment between study and practical work for Phoebe.

Cedric was also in charge of the wedding arrangements with Tembe as his backup person on the ground. Tembe and Phoebe shared an apartment in the city while they studied and became firm friends with many midnight sessions of hot chocolate and secrets shared.

As the holidays approached Eric could no longer avoid visiting his mother. He arrived to find her having a pedicure. She was more than happy to see him and he was immediately worried she had evil afoot. He gave her a small peck on her cheek and knew exactly what she had planned. He had trouble keeping his face straight as he battled to avoid her seeing the anger on his face.

"Mother, I see you are being well cared for. The house is lovely and I'm kept informed of your visitors, so I know you haven't been lonely. I'm here to talk about my wedding as I'm sure you have guessed. The kingdom is doing well under my guidance and I feel vindicated in the path—"

He stopped his dialogue for a moment as his mother rolled her eyes.

"Get on with your ego fest, my son. I'm getting really bored and need a glass or two of wine to listen to this."

Eric smiled and continued, "I might not be the king of all Africa, but the small corner falling under my reign are content and happy, even growing in wealth. Our engineering skills are being sought throughout the world and we have set up a university to train others."

"Move it along son, I still have not got my wine and you might be king, but I don't have to listen to this nonsense for ever." Atalia growled.

"The titanium on the beaches is being mined and of course the wild life is bringing in huge groups of eager eco-tourists. The cruise ships are lining up at our harbours and our youth are acting as guides and developing financial skills at the same time. Kwa-Dlangezwa, the university near Empangeni, is free from violence and for the first time in many years. Our youth are able to study with hope. I know you aren't proud of me, as you always wanted me to gather the other kingdoms under my aegis, but this works better for me. As well as the people of Zululand."

Atalia gave a fake snore as a courtier filled her glass with sparkling wine.

"Tsk tsk Eric, king of all and you can't even buy your mother real Champagne. How long must I suffer these inferior wines you foist on me?"

Eric ignored her diatribe and continued on with his own.

"Alpheus is now a key part of my government and Ragnar has become my foreign minister. My brothers are planning on moving back home so they too can take their place as princes of the kingdom as is their right."

"Huh, the worst news I've heard all year. Those useless brothers of yours will stab you in the back, the first chance they get."

"Oh Mother, you're a fine one to speak. I'm sure you wouldn't hesitate to do terrible things to get your way. Well, I do trust my brothers and sisters and for the first time ever we're spending time together, getting to know who we really are and I know we love each other as siblings should."

Taking out an ornate invitation, Eric handed his mother the card. She flicked it onto a table and totally ignored it.

"Now, let us talk about the wedding. If you attend you'll be supervised at every moment. No hidden meetings with conspirators, no vials of poison hidden in your clothing, celebrations and joy are all we want. If you cannot abide this decision then we'll make an excuse to our guests and you'll be sent somewhere safe.

"Is this not what you wanted, Mother? Me as king and ruler, getting married and having lots of little children to fill the courts with their laughter? You would be a grandmother."

Atalia pulled such a sour face Eric could not help but laugh. "Come on, Mother. You might like children who love you regardless of who you are."

"Well, as long as they are nothing like you, Eric. I suppose I could abide a few grandchildren to guide and mould. If they don't stab me in the back, after all I have done for them, like someone I could name." She glared at Eric as she said this and it made him laugh all the more.

By the time he left nothing had been settled. Eric felt a little sad his beloved father would not be at his side and his mother had taken the path she had, making her presence more of a hindrance than a joy.

CHAPTER TWENTY SEVEN

Phoebe waited for him on his return to the palace and he lifted her off her feet and swung her around, pleased to feel her sweet spirit wash over him.

"Not long now, my sweet, and we need never be apart again." He whispered into her ear as they hugged.

"Oh, Eric, I wish I could believe it, but I know one day you will grow tired of me and marry another wife or maybe even two. After all your father had five wives in total and my father has three." She teased him as she pulled away from him.

"Never. I'll never grow tired of you, Phoebe, even when you're bent with age and wrinkled beyond belief." Eric teased right back.

Ragnar came forward and laughingly informed them he had a list of possible second and third wives if it was what Eric wanted. Many of the great kingdoms of Africa had sent photos of their princesses as the Zulu kingdom grew in strength and wealth. Many lesser rulers wanted to align themselves with Eric and it was no surprise he was a sought-after husband for the young women of the land.

Over their dinner, they got down to the serious business of marriage. The Sangoma was sent for and would present himself after dessert to throw the bones to see what day would be the most fortuitous. The moon and stars had to all be in a certain position. Eric had already sent three bullocks to the Sangoma as payment for this service.

With a rattle of cowrie shells and a flick of a rawhide whip, the old man made his entrance. He sat on a leopard skin rug on the floor and carefully arranged his accoutrements around him. A skull of a monkey acted as the vessel to contain all the lesser bones to be thrown. Black and white shiny stones were arranged in a circle and the Sangoma started a deep throated hum.

Two young apprentices beat a slow rhythm on small drums. Chicken feathers dipped in a bowl of blood were thrown high in the air and everyone held their breaths as they fluttered to the ground. The Sangoma shook his head, touched one feather gently and moved another one slightly. A soft keening sound rose to the rafters and Phoebe held her breath before she took a deep gulp of air as she watched the spectacle.

Then the bones were shaken and the monkey skull raised high in the air. The Sangoma's skinny arms hung with loose skin and the claw like fingers wove their magic in the ether.

With a wild shout, the bones were ejected from the skull and scattered across the floor. Some fell within the circle of stones, while others skittered further afield. The old man took out a pouch of powder and issued a sharp grunt as he threw a pinch of powder to all four corners of the room.

"Now, my king. This feather here represents the spirit of your father. He is close at hand." He closed his eyes and sniffed the feather in question before laying it aside. Most of the other feathers had at least one piece of bone on or nearby and the Sangoma looked at each gathering carefully. Phoebe felt the hair on her arms and neck rise up as if stirred by a ghostly presence.

"Mmm, thks, thks, this one here is not good. I see a black crow hovering over this union. Someone is trying hard to destroy the joining of these two people. It will require the sacrifice of a goat of purest white at full moon my lord to shift this tagahti from your marriage."

Phoebe gripped Eric's hand and he gently rubbed his thumb over her palm as they both leaned forward, fascinated with the process of divination.

"This feather has two stones on it and it represents you as a couple. Stay close always and you will be safe. Speak to each other often, as communication is the key to success. Aaah, now this one is what we're looking for. An auspicious date and will go down in the annals of history as a great day. Third of June. Yes, very good. A lunchtime ceremony. But this black crow concerns me. I can see it creeping forward to overshadow the day. Be careful my lord, be vigilant. There are those who would pretend to be your friends and don't have your happiness at heart.

"Perhaps you should go for a cleansing before the day. I know a perfect place. A small spa in the Drakensberg Mountains and run by a lovely couple who'll treat you well. And now you, Miss Phoebe. You are surrounded by light. You see this feather here has very little blood on it, but it's surrounded by bones, you are surrounded by your family and friends. You'll be taken care of and don't need to worry."

A small bowl was brought forward and a few twigs placed in the bottom. The Sangoma lit the sticks with a magic flick of his fingers. A great puff of blue smoke hovered over the bowl as the old man fed each feather into the flames. The smell of burning feathers tickled their noses.

The drums went silent and the two young apprentices each took an arm and helped the Sangoma to his feet.

Eric put his arm around Phoebe's shoulders as they bowed to the entourage of the witchdoctor. "I honour you, Gogo. Thank you for your service and advice, we will surely listen to your council and hope to see you at the wedding in June. I will ask my advisors to shift my meetings around so I can take advantage of the spa as you suggested. Thank you."

Once the old man left and the guests moved towards their rooms for the night when Eric looked over at one of the royal guards and beckoned him over. Bending their heads close together Eric gave the man his instructions and then leaned back in his chair to await the outcome of his conversation. The guard was back with a report.

Phoebe and Ragnar both tried to hear what was said but the whispering was so quiet it was possible to only hear a word or two. With a laugh Eric recounted to them what had transpired. "I saw a friend of my mother's in the audience hall and wondered if he was on a spying mission, so I sent the guard to follow him to his room. Who wants to come with me for a chat to the gentleman in question?"

Both Phoebe and Ragnar were quick to their feet and eager to hear what was to happen. When they reached the rooms the man was on his cell phone and were embarrassed when they entered and ended his call quickly.

"Ah, Gumede, how good to see you in the palace again. I'm interested to find out your reason for visiting me. Sit at the table and we can have a good talk."

Gumede was even more nervous as Eric patted him on the shoulder in a friendly way. "Your mother has asked me to tell her what is happening in the royal courts my liege. I informed her the Sangoma had visited and a date had been set."

For the next half hour Eric plied the man with stories of the royal courts and everyone laughed at the funny activities of the extended royal family. Nieces and nephews were invited over and each child brought their own personality and idiosyncrasies.

Gumede smiled along with them but his forehead beaded with sweat and his fingers never stopped playing with the belt at his waist. No one tried to probe him for information about the Queen and he was lulled into a sense of security. Finally, Gumede could stand it no longer and blurted out the Queen planned a return to the palace and was gathering her supporters for the expected fracas.

Nkomo offered large sums of money to back her bid for the throne and Namaqua and Per were acting as go between.

The three-young people let him speak unhindered and then rose as one, they turned around and walked out without a single word of farewell. At a signal to the guard, Gumede had his cell phone removed from him and the door locked securely.

"Eric what did you put on the man's coat? It looked like a bug and not the creepy crawly type either."

"Yes, I know. I felt this day is so important I can't leave anything to chance and I asked the engineering department to make me this little bug in case I needed to use it."

Eric looked a little bit shame faced as he waited for Phoebe to say something.

"Silly, silly man, there are other ways to ensure our wedding day goes well. But I'm not cross with you, it might not be nice to spy on someone without them knowing, but I suppose I can understand your reasoning. Never spy on me. Ever. Do you understand?"

Eric hung his head for a moment before lifting his eyes and winking at Phoebe. His eyes twinkled as he nodded his head and then grabbed her in a giant hug before he whispered goodnight and headed off to his rooms.

The next morning Gumede was ushered to the gates of the kingdom and commanded not to return. He scuttled off down the road, much relieved he had not been thrown into prison for plotting against the king. He was known as a diligent and faithful worker, who found it difficult to change allegiances, but he wondered if it was time to distance himself from Atalia and her evil plans.

The advisors did not want the king to go off to the spa with the threat of his mother and her cronies hanging over their heads, but Eric happily took the road to the spa and thoroughly enjoyed his time away. He had faith his listening device would alert him to any plans to disrupt the day.

His mother made some tentative plans to boycott the wedding, but was too proud to miss the chance to socialise and see all her old cronies. His spies at the mountain home notified him of every little conversation between his mother and Raz and none of them worried him in the least. He was on cloud nine. As the day grew nearer Atalia had another change of heart and decided it would do her no good to be at the wedding. Eric shrugged his shoulders and agreed. "Whatever my Mother wants is fine by me."

The Sangoma promised Eric a momentous wedding day and he felt all was good with the world.

"The world will be in awe of your magnificence my King. Your bride will be a vision to behold and the elements of the earth will be in attendance. Even the very heavens and the stars above will be joyful at this union. Go forth and prosper my Liege. You have been blessed by nature and your ancestors stand ready on the other side of the veil of death to help you achieve your desires and dreams. Turn to them often with reverence and you will not falter or fail." The old man promised with a confident look on his aged face.

The wedding day was around the corner and Cedric and Francis frantically dashed around tasting cakes and visiting florists. Decorations were kept simple at the behest of Phoebe and her family. They wanted a wedding elegant and classy.

Phoebe asked for a week off from her studies to help with the final arrangements. Nyoni was a vision of peace and Thandi and Sarah anticipated every need the bride could have. Bridesmaids were trained on how to walk and what to do on the day. Tembe and Phoebe hid themselves in the workshops to create a wedding dress like nothing seen before.

The skirt was made of a thousand small metal feathers in white, yellow and rose gold. The bottom feathers subtly darker so the dress had an Ombre effect as it rose to the crisp white satin bodice trimmed with tiny silver butterflies. The crown, holding the veil, was simple and so finely made the best jewellers in the land would have been proud to have made it.

From head to toe, Phoebe looked like a heavenly being on a visit to an earthly realm. The bridesmaids' dresses were covered in miniature birds and butterflies so as the girls moved the skirts took flight. There were tears and tantrums, laughter and hugs as details were finalized until Nyoni could step back and say, "It's done. There is nothing more we can do now except enjoy the day."

CHAPTER TWENTY EIGHT

The day started with a gentle mist hovering over the forest. Phoebe and her bridal group sat down to a splendid breakfast before the beauticians and hair stylists arrived to primp and preen the women until not a hair was out of place. Eyes were painted with iridescent paints, lips were blotted and creams rubbed into newly pedicured feet.

Phoebe was almost too scared to move in case some young technician saw another flaw needing to be corrected. As mother of the bride, Thandi carefully arranged the veil and the adjusted the bracelets. Wiping tears and errant drops of sweat. The women of the tribe watched with pride the first of their children to make the commitment of marriage.

Eric sent a key in an envelope as his gift to Phoebe on their wedding day. Ragnar sheepishly revealed. "It is the key to a custom-made workshop created with you in mind."

Each bridesmaid was given a gift of a set of Prada bags and the flower girls were happy to receive silver crowns covered in delicately crafted enamel daisies. The girls twirled and spun until they turned a delicate shade of green the mothers knew all too well foretold a dash to the bathroom and many tears. They were asked to sit quietly for a moment and finally all was once more under control.

They sat with the filigree crowns in their hands and oohed and aahed at the pretty headdresses. Phoebe looked at the key and slipped it onto the chain around her neck. Eric knew she did not value shiny things, but a place to create her work was all she had ever hoped for. A place to call her own. The groomsmen were also given gifts tailor made especially for them.

Phoebe was glad to know this thoughtful gesture had come about without her having to prod and push Eric in any way. One final test passed by her fiancé and she could finally embrace the idea of marriage with a clear conscience.

The glade in the Nkandla forest where the wedding was to take place was groomed and trimmed, cleaned and cleaned again. Seats were brought in and a floral bower was placed where the dappled sunlight lit it up so it looked like spun gold in amongst a forest of green.

Alpheus was in his element and happily surveyed the beauty of the forest. The weather itself appeared to shine on the day. The morning mist burned off and the day could not have been any more perfect if it had been ordered on purpose. He did not notice the slither of a stealthy footstep or the silent blending of a body into the camouflage of the trees. A scratching sound like fingernails on chalk boards. A blot on the peace of the glade. He was focused on other things and missed the signs of discord.

Alpheus stroked the big Tamboti tree with reverence and admired the orchids hidden amongst the epiphytes. More beautiful than the largest cathedral, more majestic than palaces and castles, this is where he felt closest to the God of all creations and he shed a small tear before dashing it off his cheek and searched for his eldest daughter. He did not hear the leaves rustle and the forest sigh in pain, as branches were bent over and delicate plants trampled by the malevolent presence, in their haste to find the perfect hiding place for their violent scheme.

Eric and his two brothers stood at the front with Ragnar acting as best man. Resplendent in his wedding suit of a leopard skin draped over a crisp white shirt and smart dress pants. Each prince wore a similar outfit and Ragnar stood proud in a simple cloak of springbok skin.

The air held its breath as the sound of a flute floated through the trees. Alpheus stepped forward with a glorious vision of beauty and light holding his arm. Eric put his hand to his heart to stop its rapid beating as he watched Phoebe advance towards him.

He could not have explained to you what she wore, except she was the most beautiful thing he had ever seen. She smiled for him and his bones melted with love. Alpheus handed Phoebe into Eric's hands and stepped back to take his rightful place next to his wives. His smile was wide enough to make his cheeks ache and he told himself to stop looking like a silly loon. It was not like him to get sentimental at weddings but this wedding was special. It was not every day his eldest child married a king.

The bridesmaids fluttered off to the sides and the groomsmen stood tall and proud next to their assigned woman. Ten little flower girls danced around the glade, throwing white rose petals up in the air, until their little baskets were empty. A few of the female guests wiped tears off their cheeks, while the men wondered what all the fuss was about.

The ceremony went off without a hitch. No sign of a vengeful Atalia, no threat, no anger could disturb this perfect day.

"Today we are gathered here in the sight of nature and all creation to join together this man and this woman in holy matrimony." The time-tested ceremony with its familiar words and ancient cadences washed over the gathered congregation. Eric smiled down at his new wife and raised his eyebrow in a quirky salute to her beauty. Phoebe winked back at him and the two of them smiled in unison.

"You may kiss your bride." rang through the company. People stretched their necks to get a better view, when an apparition of skin, bones and anger erupted from behind a tree. E'Showe, the wood sprite chief, appeared from nowhere and everyone was taken by surprise. The feeling of love and peace was shattered as E'Showe jumped to the centre of the bower and started ranting and raving about the desecrating of the forests. His eyes shone with fevered excitement. Spittle sat like white foam on his lips and his mouth opened to spew forth a screech of anger rising through the tree canopy like a thousand harpies. As if Nature itself cried in pain, leaves shivered and diamond like dew drops fell to the ground as silent tears. Small animals quietly melted into the forest and made their way to safety. Mothers gathered their children close to their skirts and Fathers stepped forward in challenge.

No one really listened to the words of E'Showe, but if they had they would have been even more alarmed. Veins stood out on his body and you could see the blood pulsing through in hectic frantic floods. He was not looking at anyone in particular as his rhetoric of anger and hate spewed forth. He blamed everyone and anyone in a terrifying rant of vitriol. Poison emanated from every pore of his shrivelled body as he shook with adrenalin. His hand and fingers curled over a dead man's switch and those in the front of the group realised the danger as his fingers twitched and spasmed. They wondered if his frail body could sustain this energy level for much longer as he threw his arms into the air with abandon.

The royal guards were on their way to intercept the angry old man, when Alpheus held up his hand and shouted.

"Stop. He has a bomb strapped to his body." It was only then the guests realised the strapping around the bony body had a purpose. E'Showe was agitated and never stopped moving as he listed all the atrocities he was going to avenge. From the wooden table in the palace to the clearing of land for houses, his particular focus. People stood in stunned silence and for some his speech was a jumble of sounds, but for others his words cut like knives into their very being.

He brought up things done many years before Eric was even born. Forests of foreign imported trees pushing the natural forests into extinction for roads built through pristine valleys. There was no end to his list of grievances.

"No one listens, no one cares. Today everyone will listen and when I blow up the ruling family, everyone will care and maybe things will change. We'll go back to living simply. We'll find balance in nature."

While E'Showe yelled his anger to the skies, Alpheus quietly positioned himself in front of his daughter and her new husband. Thandi, Nyoni and Sandra linked arms and formed a line in front of Phoebe, Eric and their group. The family stood as a united front and Eric and his entourage were gently pushed back. Ragnar looked around to assess the best escape routes and regretted not bringing his fighting stick with him to the wedding but who would have thought he would need it on this day of love.

Phoebe kissed Eric on his cheek and whispered. "All will be well."

He hoped their guests made their escape and wished none of them would stay to see the outcome of this encounter. He was angry with himself for not seeing this threat coming. He had thought it would come from his mother, or maybe her friends, but never an obscure group from the North. His focus had been on the wrong person all along. And now it was too late to do anything.

The tirade came to an end and E'Showe came to a stop right in the centre of the glade with the large Tamboti tree towering above him. He took a deep breath. With an angelic smile on his face and a quiet sigh, he released the dead man switch and the air around him caught fire on this perfect day. Eric looked around and saw the skies darken, the foliage shred and fly all around him without a single piece touching him. The noise was so horrendous, and Eric was sure he was dead and this was all a strange moment in time. He looked around for his wife and even his brothers and Ragnar. The air still shivered with light and fire, but not a sign of even a single injury. What he had not seen was Alpheus lift up his beautifully carved fighting stick and cry out to the forests around them.

"Forests of my ancestors, trees nourishing my heart and my soul, protect those I love." And with this simple invocation he brought his fighting stick down and touched it to the ground in reverence. A force greater than explosives, mightier than the anger of an old man, surged through the earth and encompassed the people in the grove. The air itself shivered as the energy of the towering trees spread forth and covered all within its reach, apart from the destruction of the bomb wielding zealot. The energy of his weapon was focused on the one spot around him. It vented itself straight up into the sky. A few branches and leaves took the brunt of the devastation but nothing totally destroyed.

Time stood still as E'Showe was consumed and reduced to the dust of eternity in a moment. He did not scream and his spirit exited this life with barely a sigh. The hands of his ancestors reached through the veil of death to pluck him into the world of Spirits with a murmur and a sigh.

If anyone watched him they would have seen a look of surprise and shock on his face as he accepted his self-inflicted fate. He then burnt up and vanished in a flash of light. Gone forever but not forgotten by those he had affected with his vitriolic tirade. Where once he had occupied life with anger, now he was gone, leaving barely a ripple in the fabric of time.

When the fire and flying debris had abated the guests appeared from behind bushes and trees shocked and upset. The little flower girls handed their baskets to some of the young men and sharp splinters were collected and disposed of. The men worked quietly and efficiently until the glade looked safe once more. Some of the children quietly cried into their mothers' skirts and some of those same mothers bit their lips in an effort to control their own shock. Fathers found they could take control and hustled their families like a shepherd with his sheep. Trying not to show their own shock and fear, they grunted and grumbled about the cost of clothes dirtied in the effort to find refuge.

"Neat trick, Alpheus. I can see you'll be a father-in-law I should be careful not to annoy." laughed the relieved groom.

People started to laugh in relief and Alpheus clapped his hands loudly.

"We have a marriage to celebrate people. The festivities will continue at my kraal. The groomsmen will lead the way and the bride and groom will be right behind them. Come along, friends and family, let's leave the forest and walk into the light."

Ragnar took one last look at the scorched earth around the bower. There was no sign of the old man or the beautifully decorated wedding arbour, but there was also no sign of injury or lasting hurt to anyone except for the tragic figure of E'Showe. Ragnar happily took Tembe by the hand and led the way down the path. It had certainly been a day to remember.

The wedding reception was much more subdued than planned and many people whispered to their loved ones how much they appreciated them. Husbands hugged wives, siblings apologised for ancient hurts and the children ran riot with gay abandon.

Eric took Phoebe off to a quiet spot and the two of them had a silent tear as they considered the day they had experienced. Alpheus stood at the table and called out to the couple to join him. "No time for crying my children, only a little bit longer and then you may go your own way."

A huge cake was rolled forth and food had tables groaning as speeches were called for. Ragnar recounted stories of boyhood mishaps and people slowly relaxed as the mood changed from shock to safety.

Tembe sat with the elephant soldiers and loud laughter rang forth as she teased them about their love lives. Alpheus danced with Rachel and Maria and spun the younger children round until they cried with joy. Phoebe went off to change her clothes with her bridesmaids in attendance, she returned dressed in a simple shift dress flowed around her in a bell shape. She sat down on a chair fashioned from the vines of the forest and adorned with blossoms Francis had decorated for this moment.

Claude, Cedric and Ragnar lifted her up high in the air and paraded her through the guests. She gripped the sides of the chair as friends and family jostled for a closer spot. She had a small posy of flowers in her lap and with a hoot and a yell she threw it into the pack of unmarried girls. Arms and legs flew as the girls scrambled for the prize. Leaves and petals were stripped from the posy as the melee got more and more competitive. The girl, who stood triumphant, dashed around the dance floor with her friends racing after her to try and grab the bouquet. The beautiful little posy now looked more like a few sparse sticks and only a single daisy survived to wobble its head in defiance.

Next it was the turn of the young men and Eric carefully removed the frilly garter from Phoebe's thigh and twirled it around his finger. He jumped on a table and pulled the elastic back until Phoebe thought the delicate item may snap but then he released it over the heads of the crowd with a zing. It flipped through the air and caught on an errant breeze as it fluttered over the heads of the jumping young men to finally land on the surprised head of Francis. He had quietly sat at a table and was watching the craziness of the wedding traditions with a feeling of love for those around him but with no desire to join in the clamour and scramble.

Cedric immediately put down the chair leg he held and dashed to his partner. Phoebe wobbled slightly on her perch until Cele stepped into the breach and took the weight of the chair. Cedric jumped in Francis' lap as the crowd erupted in cheers.

The guests started a slow clap as Cedric and Francis regally paraded around the tables and held aloft the frilly green garter in their joined hands.

Some of the older families readied to leave. Children nodded off and parents gathered them up for the trip home. It was the perfect time for the bride and groom to leave and Eric signalled for Ragnar to bring the car around. A corridor of aunts and uncles demanded final kisses and friends wished them good fortune as they lined the path to the car. Finally, the couple could leave for their honeymoon. But then the car stuttered and stalled as it came to a definite and abrupt stop. Ragnar scratched his head, but Phoebe was sure she saw a glitter of mischief in his eyes as he urged them to exit the motor vehicle.

"Sorry guys. Looks like we'll have to find another mode of transport. Any suggestions friends?"

Everyone looked around in confusion when Claude came out of the forest with a brightly coloured wheelbarrow and a pretty pink pillow in its base, pushing it forward with a squeak.

"Will this do?"

Everyone laughed heartily at this and Phoebe gracefully sat in this new carriage and winked at Ragnar and Claude.

"Cheeky boys. What am I going to do with you?"

Eric spat on the palms of his hands, shrugged his shoulders and with a grunt he picked up the handles of the wheelbarrow. "Wife if this is to be our mode of transport from now on, we might have to cut back on the wedding cake a little bit."

He pushed his blushing bride down the pathway and away from the guests. The clatter of tin cans tied to the wheelbarrow could be heard long after they had vanished from view. Ragnar and Claude clapped each other on their backs, happy with this final little bit of fun. The day had been retrieved from disaster and no one would ever forget this   wedding.

EPILOGUE

Atalia sat on her comfortable couch and scowled at Raz as he advised her of the wedding including all the relevant gossip. She flicked an invisible piece of dust off her clothes as she listened. Instead of feeling happy her only child's marriage had started without serious injury to her family, she felt a black cloud of anger engulf her.

"Stupid fool, E'showe, underestimated Alpheus. If he had listened to me he would've had a lot more explosives around the perimeter. Maybe even some sharp shooters hidden in the trees. A carefully placed bullet or two no one could see coming would have been perfect. This is what comes of having fanatics do the dirty work, they always have to explain everything. More bang, bang and less rant, rant would have been my advice."

Raz nodded his head in agreement as Atalia ripped the flower petals from an undeserving innocent orchid.

"Raz call the troops. We need to plan for the future."

Atalia took out her lipstick and applied her trademark red lipstick onto pursed lips as she looked out the window at the waning moon and sighed.

CHECK THIS OUT

If you liked this book you might like this as well.

Praise for Blazing Blunderbuss by Nix Whittaker

This novel is a unique blend of high fantasy and
steampunk adventure- **Steampunk Cavalier**

ISBN Soft Cover, 978-0-473-41313-2
ISBN Kindle,978-0-473-41314-9

PLEASE WRITE REVIEWS

If you loved this book please leave a review. Authors live or die on good reviews so even a few words would be greatly appreciated.

ABOUT THE AUTHOR

Patricia Pike was born in South Africa and moved to New Zealand to give her family a brighter future. She is also an artist and has written and illustrated children's books and adult colouring in books. If you would like to know more or to contact Patricia please visit her website at https://reshwity.wixsite.com/patriciapike